Skin That Screams

Thomas Stewart

BAYNAM BOOKS PRESS

Book Cover Christy Aldridge

Editor Sidney Shiv

Praise for Skin that Screams

"Skin that Screams is a collection of short stories centring around body horror. Each story was unique and absolutely terrifying. I felt like I was in a continuous nightmare that intensified as I progressed forward. I really enjoyed Thomas's writing style throughout the book, and I truly felt as if I was physically there from beginning to end. While I enjoyed every single one of these stories, my favorite was the closing story, Jared's other half. Thank you, Thomas, for allowing me to be an ARC reader for you. Now, I'll be diving into some of your other stories, that I have not yet had the pleasure of reading."

-- Goodreads

"I'm usually not into short stories. But this was amazing. Creepy. Sick. Disturbing. I loved it."

-- Dal R., *The Lady In White*

"Highly recommend it. Please make sure you read the trigger warnings."

"OMG!!! ok so this book was all sorts of insane.... in an amazing way. There was everything i love about splatter punk in here. Gore, blood, guts, grossness, and so much more. The short stories just kept getting better and better. I have few favourites, but I won't spoil it for anyone. His writing style was phenomenal. Definitely one on my top 10 favorites. as i read i could see the images playing out and it was .... disgusting. 10 out of 10 recommend!"

-- Goodreads

"*Skin That Screams* by Thomas Stewart is a collection of nightmare tales forcing readers to face their greatest fear

– themselves. Stewart writes, about "misery … just being deadlocked in a state of entropy … unable to move or do anything to help yourself …" This is the detritus of our nightmares, those rotting, decaying, niggling questions living inside your skin that come to life at 3AM when you can't sleep. *Skin That Screams* is the perfect title for this book. All the stories deal with characters wanting to escape their skin.

If we could escape our own skin, we could escape society's ego, our vanity, our lover, our monster, and our obsession with our bodies. In "Plastique Wipes," "Hunnyfresh," "After Party," and "Jared's Other Half", we take journeys of truth and discovery. If I'm younger and more attractive, do I have more value? If I'm skinnier and lose just a few pounds faster, will I feel more beautiful? If I can cut this ugly part of myself out that nobody sees but me, will the monster inside me go away? Stewart uses the body horror subgenre to force us to look at these frequent questions.

Stewart uses simple language with frightful descriptions and fast-paced scenes, keeping the reader engaged in the gross horror of the moment. It is also hard to write a review of a body horror collection when Thomas Stewart so bravely shares his own struggles with anorexia and bulimia at the beginning of the book—all these stories of transmogrification deal with adding or taking an aspect of yourself away. If you haven't read this book, I hope you do. At least it will help you find a bit of yourself or a good scream under the covers."

-- Nora B. Peevy, *Hellnotes*

This book has some creative body horror. It's a realistic approach from everyday privileges that will disturb you. Your skin will crawl as the writer puts you in those scenarios with perspective writing. You'll never look at common things again. A must-read for body horror!

-- Post-Mortem author of *'Us' and ' Written in Carnage'*

Dedication

This tome is dedicated strictly to both myself and my beloved maggots and larvae. Conceited as that may sound, allow me to explain. I dedicate this to you all, as your praise and adulation for my previous title, The Homicidal Artists, helped significantly get me to want to do another project such as this one. As I've explained before, that volume served as a challenge to see how many words I could write in a single day and to write the stories from start to finish in a single day.

It was incredibly fun for me, and you all seemed to enjoy it, so of course, I just had to do it again! But now, for the part where I must dedicate myself to this. Though The Homicidal Artists inspired me in this with its method and execution, I want you all to know the theme of these stories carries a bit of a personal drive with me. I purposely chose the theme of straight body horror, as I, myself, have suffered personal body horror in real life in the forms of anorexia and bulimia nervosa. For years, my body image has plagued me both mentally and physically, destroying me slowly, as well as those closest to me. These things have taken from me some of my happiest memories and relationships and have, in part, led to the diseased imagination that has plagued you for three years.

I will say, though, that I feel somewhat comfortable in claiming that I am currently starting to recover from these ailments, and writing horror has also had a significant role in this. To those who've been by my side throughout my career as a demon scribe of the macabre, I hope now you see and realize just how much I could never thank you enough for doing so. Your genuine words have provided me with more peace in my passion and life than much of anything in the past three years. For this, you will always carry my eternal love and gratitude.

-- Thomas S.

Contents

My Body's Screaming

I'm writing this because I know it won't be long before I no longer can. It's becoming too painful, mostly physically, to write any of this.

A skin condition—that's how this all started. Fucking itchy bumps, like chicken pox or some shit, you know? Shit you don't even think would be a problem. Just apply some ointment and go on with your day, right?

Well, I tried that, and you know what? It didn't do a damn thing! Hell, I think it might've even made it worse! I felt sick as a damn dog, too, constantly sweating, feeling like my organs weren't organs at all but lead weights. I couldn't even eat anything without choking it all back up because of the way it got caught in my throat. That's another thing—I can barely breathe right now.

Anyway, this first started happening about two weeks ago. I'd just gotten back from a cruise, putting my three thousand dollar bonus from work to good use. When I woke up the next day, I felt like absolute shit. Imagine every hangover you've ever had, and then imagine somebody's filled your body with jelly. Trying to move my arms or legs felt like I'd need a crane to lift them. What's worse is that running the lengths of my arms and legs were these great big blisters, round and yellow.

I thought at first I must've overdone it in the sun. Well, that's just it. Never mind that I'd all but bathed in SPF

5,000; it didn't actually hurt. If it were sunburn, I'd have been burning all over, right? But no, instead, everything itched like crazy. I probably looked like a crackhead the way I was picking and peeling away at myself. Even though I scratched to the point of bleeding, I still felt itchy!

Believe it or not, I exhausted myself, scratching and picking myself apart. Yes, that's right, I tired myself out by essentially tearing myself apart. That, too, was probably the only kind of relief I got during any of this.

When I woke up, so did the pain and itching. Thanks to the pain from what I'd done to myself, I couldn't even move to scratch anywhere. I couldn't scratch, couldn't get out of bed, nothing. That, I think, was when the word "misery" was redefined for me—being deadlocked in a state of entropy, unable to move or do anything to help myself.

I remember trying to close my eyes again. A small part of me figured that maybe I'd wake up, and whatever this was would pass like a stomach bug or something. Perhaps I'd wake up and find this was all just a weird dream, right?

Ha ha, *HELL NO!*

I couldn't fall asleep because I was in so much pain. So I couldn't even get relief again. This was when I realized shit was serious and that if I didn't get help, I'd likely rot right there in my bed, and that was if this condition or whatever didn't somehow get me first. With the most effort it's ever taken me, I managed to force my right arm to grab my phone and dial an ambulance. The entire time I was on the phone, every inch of my body was pricked by thousands of itches. It felt like at least two hives' worth of pissed-off hornets were coming down on top of me.

They told me they were about three to five minutes out, and you best believe those were some of the worst fucking three to five minutes of my life. However, despite all of this, all the pain and agony I've just described, this is just the start of things getting freaky. I started hearing a faint whistling noise, like the sound from my tea kettle every morning. Soft and distant as it was, I thought it was just my ears ringing or something.

Then it started to escalate, building in pitch like whoever it was was getting closer to me. The closer and louder it got, the more I noticed it started to echo. Not only that, but... But I think I began hearing *words!*

I couldn't tell *what* they might've been saying, but I knew it was something. Suddenly, a sharp pain, the kind I could only imagine from being flayed alive or vivisected awake, shot across my entire body from my stomach. That had to have been the loudest I've ever screamed before, and it tore my vocal cords in half. By the time I stopped, I'd lost my voice entirely, which I still haven't recovered from.

Several more pains like this erupted across my chest and back. I could've sworn I was having my skin peeled from my bones, slowly and almost intimately, like by a serial killer or something. When I forced my head up to see exactly what it was, I realized the reality was far worse.

Across my body were enormous, almost cavernous-looking gashes, opened wide and seemingly yawning. They puckered back and forth horizontally. This was when the screaming became deafening. Quickly putting two and two together, I knew this had to be what they were coming from, too. My body was *literally* screaming now.

Eventually, the paramedics came crashing through the front door, likely having heard my shrieking (which, being honest, I'm almost convinced could be heard from the next town over), and flooded into my bedroom. The look of pure shock and horror on their faces when they got an eyeful of me, of what's become of my body, is one I'll never forget. One of the EMT's jaws almost fell off of his face and crashed to the floor while the others turned and did everything possible not to empty their stomachs all over my floor.

All of this barely registered with me because, by this time, my ears were tone-deaf from the screaming. It sounded like I was in the middle of the street during a protest or something—pure pandemonium. When I didn't see any of the paramedics reacting to the noise, I realized I was the only one hearing this.

Collecting and, as best they could, steeling themselves, the paramedics lifted me from the bed onto a stretcher. Though I could tell they were *trying* to be gentle, it didn't feel like it. Despite this, I was wheeled out of there, out of my house, and into the back of an ambulance.

During my ride to the hospital, I heard the whispering voices again, and this time, I began discerning certain words. It was all jumbled. I could only make out phrases such as *"Skin"* and *"plastic"* and stuff like *"other half"* or *"food."* None of it made any sense, but the longer I listened, the more and more I began to hear.

This was two weeks ago. The doctors have told me that what's happened is something they've never seen or encountered. Yeah, no fucking shit, Sherlock.

They say they're "working round the clock" to figure out how to fix this—if that's even remotely possible, whatever *this* is. I can tell you right now that *this* isn't some "skin condition" and definitely not a sunburn. I may not know what it is, but it sure as hell isn't either of those.

Another thing I'll say, and this is the other reason I'm having to type this, is that these screams aren't just random, disembodied voices. I have no clue who the voices belong to, but I know that whoever they are, they're in tremendous agony, just like me. There are so many voices I lost count.

Over the past five or six days, I've listened to them scream stories, horrific ones about kids, with people tearing their way out of their bodies, people turning into creatures just barely reminiscent of human beings in a science lab, and even one about a man who was found with his stomach blown out from something bursting out into the free world. All of these were enough to give me nightmares for the next couple of nights, and those were just the nights I *did* manage to close my eyes and fall asleep.

And whenever I do, the pain of my body goes away. But each time I wake up...

My body is still screaming at me!

New Menu Item

W endall looks up at the clock, having seen the sun
go down. 6:30 P.M. He sighs.

Only 6:30. Great...

The past two hours have been completely dead at Burger Castle—not a single order. With all the extra time, the crew has already managed to pretty much take care of everything that the general manager and corporate constantly bitch at them about, including scrubbing the shit out of the baseboards to the point where the paint is chipping off. And still, not a single goddamn order. Oh, and of course, they could forget about asking to close early.

"We need to make all the money we can," management would say. Two dollars and fifty cents—the approximate profits they'd rake in from the two orders they'd gotten all afternoon.

Fuckin' clowns.

Wendall looks back at his phone, scrolling through his FaceBook feed, when one of the cooks calls for him. He looks up, giving him the most tired look possible. "What do you want, Chris?"

"Hey, we were wondering..." he begins.

"No," Wendall blurts, already knowing where this is going.

"Bro, can you let me finish?"

He sighs, drops his head, and gestures for Chris to continue.

"So me and the others were thinking, you wanna try this new burger they're coming out with next week?"

Wendall frowns. "Huh?"

"Yeah, you haven't heard?"

"Heard what, dude?" He asks impatiently.

"Okay, so check it." He digs out his phone and begins flipping through various Facebook posts. He stops on Burger Castle's latest post, which features a picture of the most enormous burger either has ever seen. "See that?" he exclaims loudly.

Wendall shrugs and replies, "Yeah, so?"

"Bruh, you're telling me that don't look awesome to you?"

"Not really, man. Besides, I'm vegetarian. Burgers don't impress me, especially not the ones getting shat out of here." Chris sighs exasperatedly.

'Well, anyway," Chris continues, his voice noticeably less excited than earlier. "It's called the Royal Pounder, and it's this big ass burger, made with at least six different meats, I think, with a *fuck* ton of condiments and shit slapped on it."

Wendall snickers.

"What?" asks Chris.

"Royal Pounder? Really?"

"Yeah... What's wrong with—"

"Who the hell came up with *that*? Jesus, maybe you should tell 'em next time not to come up with marketing ploys while they've got boners."

Chris's eyes cross. "Huh?"

'Nothing, dude. Look, whatever's the deal with this burger, I'm not interested."

"Oh, come on, man," Chris whines.

Wendall sighs. From the corner of his eye, he catches the briefest glimpse of the clock, seeing that it's only 6:45. His head drops, hanging limp from his neck. Why couldn't it be 11:30 already?

Picking his head up, Wendall looks tiredly back at Chris and says, "Alright, go on then. What's the deal with this burger?"

"Well, the thing is, the Royal Pounder—" He stops, hearing Wendall snickering again. After a quick glare, he continues, "It ain't supposed to come out till next week, right?"

Wendall nods blankly.

"Well..." Chris' eyes dart back and forth between Wendall and the meat freezer.

"What?" asks Wendall.

"Remember last week's truck?"

"Yeah, and? Look, man, I'm trying to humor you here. I'm tired, annoyed, and I *really* wanna go home. Okay? So just spit it ou—"

"Bro, I'm trying to tell you we got some of the stuff for it in the freezer!"

"Again, I ask, *and*?"

"Well, the other cooks and I wanted to see if you wanted to try it with us—get a preview of it, you know?"

"Are you nuts!" exclaims Wendall so loudly that the three other cooks turn to see what's happening. "You're trying to get me fired, is that it?"

"What? No dude, I—"

"Look, whatever I've done to you, I'm sorry, okay? You don't need to go trying to rope me into something stupid like this."

"Bro, what the fuck're you even yelling at me for? I just wanted to be nice and offer you a chance at something. You don't have to get all jumpy with me."

"I'm not jumpy. I'm telling you, you're gonna get us all in HUGE trouble doing something like this."

"How?"

"How?" repeats Wendall, scoffing. "How about getting caught stealing food? You think about that?"

"The hell are you talking about, 'stealin' food?' Dude, we get one free meal, right?"

"Yeah, but that's... That's for... You know—shit that's *actually* on the menu. You said that this hasn't even hit the market yet. What if Jason finds out we've been taking food before it's supposed to come out?"

"Come on, man, you know good and damn well as I do, he ain't gonna do fuck all."

Wendall's lips purse. He wants to say something, tell Chris to quit bullshitting. But he also knows, chances are, he'd be right anyway. Hell, Burger Castle already has the reputation of being the place that accepts everybody, from pill heads to sex offenders and even a serial killer (Well, okay, maybe not quite that extreme, even if it *did* happen once. Everyone has to learn somehow...)

Defeated, Wendall sighs and says, "Okay, look, I already said I'm not interested, okay? Y'all wanna gorge yourselves on that shit, be my guest, I won't stop you." Chris whoops and turns to bolt off to the freezer but gets stopped by Wendall's hand on his shoulder.

"But listen here, I ain't takin' no bullet for this, you got me?"

Chris attempts to shrug him off and keep going, but Wendall keeps his grip firm. "Fine, we won't say nothin' about you," Chris says.

Reluctantly, Wendall lets go of Chris's shoulder, and Chris takes off like a jackrabbit that's snorted at least six lines of coke.

Turning back around, Wendall stares out through the window in front of him. Behind him in the kitchen, he can hear the others cheering and hollering, excited to try this new beast of a burger. Wendall shakes his head.

Dumbasses. Better be SOME burger.

"Alright, the camera rolling?" Chris asks. Teresa holds up her phone and a thumbs up. "'Kay, everybody, this's Chris Reynolds at Burger Castle, and today, you're about to see me take on the brand new Royal Pounder!"

He stops for a second, allowing his coworkers to let out their cheers. He holds the burger, which he's barely able to hold with one hand, and smiles. "This is it, right here." He puts the burger up to the camera, almost smooshing it against the lens. "See that? It looks good, don't it?"

"C'mon, Chris!" shouts Ronnie.

"Yeah, Chris, let's see you take a bite!" Cheers Teresa.

Chris, absolutely high with adrenaline, unhinges his jaws and stuffs a heaping mouthful of the burger into his mouth. It's almost too much for him to chew, having to slip small sips of his cola to wash some of it down. When he's able to chew it properly, he savors every bite.

"How is it?" asks Teresa.

"Mm, Mhm!" Chris responds, mouth stuffed and nodding while holding up his thumb. It takes some extra effort for him to swallow, but finally, he does and smiles. Teresa and Ronnie let out hearty whoops while Chris washes the rest of it down with his drink.

"So, what'd it taste like?" asks Ronnie.

"Bro, I could taste every type of meat: beef, chicken, pork, the Bambi, fish, I think, and the—" His speech dies abruptly as he rubs his stomach.

Teresa chuckles and asks, "You okay there?"

"Huh? Oh, yeah, just..." He starts to grimace, clutching his stomach tighter and tighter. Soon, he's forced to double over before his eyes snap wide open. "Oh shit, I gotta go!" He bolts as fast as his legs can carry him to the bathroom.

The second he enters, he launches into the stall and fixes himself onto the commode in a single motion. He waits for the inevitable storm that's bound to come out, judging from the pain in his stomach, but nothing gives. *The hell?* He wonders.

About five minutes pass, and nothing, not even a scrap or smidgeon of shit comes out, so he starts moving to get off when the pain kicks in again, forcing him right back down on the toilet. Once again, he waits, and again, nothing happens. When he tries a second time to move, the pain kicks in again, this time a thousand times worse. Before, it felt like he might've only had a bad case of the runs, but now, it's more akin to someone driving an ice sickle into his ass and grinding his organs loose.

He yelps and cries in absolute pain. He feels his organs twist, then dissolve like melted candle wax. When he opens his eyes again, it's to the horror of his hands turning a sickly, disgusting, and downright unnatural shade of brown. It was happening all over his body, too, as he began to see, to his boundless detriment.

He screams in pain as sheer panic takes the driver's seat on his train of thought. At that moment, he hears the water in the toilet splash with something coming out of him. It feels like a rushing, crushing waterfall coming out from under him. More than this, he starts to feel lighter and lighter the more he uncontrollably empties himself.

"W-Wendall!" he wails. "Ronnie, Teresa, *somebody!*"

No one responds. No one can hear him. The walls of the restrooms are thick, built with layers of bricks and cement.

He doubles over again, feeling something eating through his stomach. His stomach was empty, devoid of the burger he'd just masticated—along with any and everything else he'd eaten—and now digesting itself from the inside out. His skin feels like it is somehow trying to eat itself, dissolving more and more by the second.

Finally, his screams and groans die away, and the bathroom falls completely silent. Slumped over on top of the toilet, Chris's body melts, dissolving entirely into a liquid resembling the fryer grease in the kitchen.

"Hey, either of you two seen Chris?" Wendall asks.

Teresa shakes her head while Ronnie shrugs.

"Not since he took off for the bathroom," Ronnie replies.

Wendall sighs and says, "Okay, I'm gonna check on him." He turns and heads for the restroom. He grits his teeth as he goes, trying to hold himself together enough not to fly off the handle at Chris. *Goddamn it, man, I fuckin' TOLD you not to do this shi--*

His thoughts die immediately upon opening the bathroom door. Foul miasma pollutes his nostrils, and he's forced to back out of the bathroom and run back to the front counter for the Lysol spray kept in the cabinet under the register. He returns and bombs the room with a cloud of aromatic fragrance before calling out, "Yo, Chris. Are you alright in here?"

He's met with complete silence. The Lysol dissipates almost as soon as it can settle, and Wendall is forced to gag again. Through watery eyes, he sees that the stall door is cracked, so he approaches it and is met with a sight more horrifying than any nightmare he's ever had or any movie he's ever seen.

In front of him on the commode, leaning forward toward him sits the bleached white skeleton of his former coworker. Dripping from the bones is like grease drops, forming an ever-growing pool around the commode. The only thing identifying the skeleton as Chris is the Burger Castle uniform hanging loose from the bones and the discarded hat, lying soaked in juice on the floor.

Wendall runs out and tells the others to evacuate the building before dialling 911. Not five minutes pass before police and first responders arrive at the restaurant.

"This just in, local burger joint, Burger Castle, has just been temporarily closed down after one of the employees was found dead in the restroom." The camera cuts to a young camerawoman standing outside of Burger Castle.

"This is Rachel Deetz, and I am standing outside Burger Castle with the restaurant staff. Beside me is the shift manager, Wendall Micheals, who supposedly found the body of his coworker, twenty-seven-year-old Christopher Farth, in the men's restroom. Tell me, what was your first clue that something was wrong?"

The microphone is handed to a distraught, petrified Wendall. With a shaking voice, he says, "H-He ran to the bathroom after trying this new burger, the Royal Pounder. He was in there for almost thirty minutes before I went to check on him. When I got in there, though…" He begins to hyperventilate, and the camera cuts back to the newsroom.

"No charges have been filed against the General Manager, Jason Ryers, or Danver Foods Inc. for the death of Christopher, but the possibility is likely. We are being told, however, that Burger Castle is being closed down for the immediate future until the definitive cause of death is determined and proper measures are ensured.

At this time, the biggest question on everyone's mind is: just what was in that Royal Pounder burger?"

"Plastique Wipes"

R ita stops scrolling through her phone, and her eyes widen. Midway through her FaceBook feed is a post reading:

"Trial run for brand new Dollface beauty care set. Limited-time beta offer, only $0.99!"

She can't believe her eyes. *Dollface?* she wonders. *THE Dollface!*—as in, the multi-million dollar beauty care company whose products go for at least a small fortune?! She clicks the post and sees their Barbie doll-face-looking logo, which confirms her belief. However, she still can't believe it. This is too good to be true. There has to be a catch, right?

She begins scrolling through the ad, eventually stumbling across the website. Funny enough, despite being a so-called "multi-million dollar company," the website appears bland and basic to Rita. I guess that profit goes toward the secret ingredients of their stuff, right?

Either that or a secret miracle formula.

Rita sets down her phone, looking out the cafe window while sipping her coffee. *Free beauty care set...* The thought circles in her mind the way water circles the drain in a bathtub. Briefly, she sees her reflection in the window. More accurately, she sees the face of the bland, mediocre, tired, full-time nine-to-fiver she's become. She thinks about all the times she joked with her friends about how they'd never let their lives end up this way, the way their parents had.

And yet, here she was, the very same, working a dead-end job as a cashier at the local mega mall across the street from the cafe. The appearance of the place accentuated this image of her in her mind, making her appear more aged than she was. She had devoted over a year and a half to that place, and for what? To come home every night and scramble for her wine cooler and down at least two full glasses to knock her out just so she could have the privilege of waking up and repeating the process the next day...

God, why couldn't I have tried that modeling gig, she wonders while gritting her teeth. Her hand clenches slightly. *Damn it, Ma, why couldn't you have just let me go for it?*

A brief instant rushes by when her mother's words return to her: *"You ain't gonna get by with your looks forever, honey. You need to have a real job and get some experience so you don't end up like me, relying on a whole bunch of men to take care of you."*

What's so wrong with that, though?

She sighs, downing the last gulp of her coffee while looking at her watch. She has another twenty minutes to kill before her shift at the mega-mart sucks the rest of her day away from her. Twenty minutes, she thinks bitterly. *And it'll all be used praying that tonight, something would happen that'd let me go home early.*

She closes her eyes and takes a cleansing breath. *Calm down. Don't think about it. Think about something else. Think about...*

Her eyes snap open. She turns around and sees her phone again, the ad still displayed on her screen. *Yeah... This works!* Snatching the phone up, she starts scrolling through the ad again, feverishly searching for the details of the giveaway. Finally, she strikes gold.

"To claim this offer, fill out the form below and check your email for further instructions."

Without missing a beat, Rita clicks on the link, redirecting her to a Google form that she fills out in under twenty seconds. It is almost all basic fare—simple questions about her height, weight, the last time she had surgery (which isn't applicable in her case), and any prior experience she might've had in modeling or testing beauty products. It isn't until the last part of the questionnaire that she is forced to pause for a moment.

"Have you or a loved one ever had any history of stage fright?"

Below this are the "Yes" or "No" options, nothing else. There are no other options, no explanations, and no fine print. Rita raises an eyebrow in suspicion. It's just a simple question.

She stares at the words for another five seconds before cautiously pressing the "No" option. After that, she submits the form before checking her watch again. Five minutes left. The form tells her that the submission has gone through and asks if she'd like to submit another response. She exits the form and FaceBook before stashing the phone away in her purse and getting up, leaving her empty cup and a ten-dollar bill on the table.

She approaches the mega mart with a slightly more enthusiastic stride. It's the little things, isn't it? The day will probably be hell, of course, but even still...

Maybe *something* good could happen now, right?

She clocks in about three minutes before the official time (which is only two minutes later than she usually clocks in, though still later than that old bat, Mrs. Hatter, wants her there—fuckin' company preferences.) and takes up her position at the register. From there, the hours almost immediately slow to a snail's crawl. Not a great sign. Still, she tries to keep her chin held high.

Think of the offer. Think of Dollface...

Customers begin coming and going, most of whom either harass her to accept their expired coupons, threaten to call corporate on her for "being rude" (translated: "She won't say 'Hi' to me and listen to me ramble about my life woes for twenty fuckin' minutes."), or ignore her existence altogether until she tells them their total. You know, the usual.

Finally, lunch break rolls around, and she clocks out and slips to the break room with a bag of chips and a Monster. When she looks at her phone, sure enough, the email from Dollface is there, greeting her with, "Congratulations for signing up as a beta tester for the Dollface UltraCare set." She opens the notification while simultaneously opening up her Doritos and chowing down.

The email itself is comprised, more or less, of the same details as the FaceBook post, with the exception being an all-new bit about participants receiving a one hundred dollar cash prize PLUS a year's subscription to all of Dollface's ongoing deals and promotions. Her eyes grow at this. One hundred dollars AND a year of discounts on some of the best beauty products on the market–*sign me up!*

At the bottom is an invoice, telling her that her package will arrive around noon that Monday. *Only a four-day wait,* she thinks. *That's not too bad.* With only another couple of minutes left of her lunch, she begins looking through the catalog, seeing the models, fantasizing that she would be one of the gorgeous faces in the photos.

Dozens of young beauty models, all with before and after photos display on the screen. Below them is a video. With five minutes left, Rita clicks on the video and immediately loses her mind with the array of products advertised as part of the package. Everything, from scented lotion (lemon, obviously -- *only her favorite*) to fragrant perfumes, candy-scented masks, and even a vanilla-scented candle thrown in just because. All of this is enough to make her heart start cutting backflips in her chest, but the coup de gras is when the video teases a "secret addition."

What this addition is isn't touched on at all. The video ends just as Rita's break does. She sighs, letting reality sink in again while throwing away her trash and putting away her phone. Just before leaving the break room, she looks at the clock. *3:45. Only another four hours.*

She briefly remembers the invoice. How ironic... She's only four days from receiving a free, top-of-the-line experimental beauty care set, and she's not sweating it. Yet four hours suddenly feel like an eternity at work—the way time can both fly and crawl.

And crawl, they do. Admittedly, a part of her is grateful that this results in a slight lack of patrons, which in turn means a lack of assholes to deal with. If only it didn't also come with prolonging her work day. Finally, though, the shift ends, and she's free to clock out and go home. She takes her things and dashes out of the mega-mart. The sun is already going down. The day is already over and giving way to night.

On her drive home, a billboard catches her attention. Who could've guessed that, of all things, it was a Dollface ad? "Try our new *Malibu Babe* lotion" is the message printed over a smokin'-hot blonde whose face looks like it's molded and sculpted from clay, finely sanded, with no rough calluses or blemishes. If only *she* could look so perfect.

Four more days... Four more days...

For the next three days, these words serve as her motto. Any time a customer mouths off to her or a coworker gives her shit, she repeats her little mantra while imagining herself on the cover of *Cosmopolitan*.

(Hell, if the stuff's really good like they say it is, she'll be on the cover of Time or Forbes, won't she?)

Finally, delivery day comes, and Rita doesn't think it can come any slower. She waits at the door the way a small puppy does when it anticipates its master coming home, ready to jump for joy at the sound of footsteps on the porch. Her heart does just this when she suddenly hears heavy footsteps clomping on the porch outside. She fights the urge to swing the door open and tackle the delivery man. She waits for the thud of her package hitting the porch—

(*"Christ, easy with all that! God, I hope they haven't broken anything."*)

—before jerking the door open as the poor bastard is about to ring the doorbell.

The FedEx guy, a kid who can't be a day over twenty-two or twenty-three (and that's stretching it), looks startled at Rita for a moment before outstretching his shaking hand with the tablet for her to sign. Without a word, Rita overzealously snatches the tablet from his hands and scrawls her name with her finger, disregarding dignity, manners, and the stylus, just to sign the damn thing and take her package.

The document is signed, and Rita snatches the package, scurrying inside and slamming the door in the kid's bewildered face. Immediately, she begins tearing the package open like it's Christmas morning, revealing a medium-sized box with the Dollface logo staring back at her. Without missing a beat, Rita opens the box and pulls out its contents. Everything advertised was there: the lotion, shampoo, scented masks, and yes, even the candle.

As she upturns the box, just to be sure, a small pamphlet falls out. Picking it up, Rita reads the following message:

"Thank you, valued customer or newcomer, for taking part in this brand-new experiment for a brand-new product. In this package, you have received the promised bundle of Dollface's latest and greatest products and an all-new, never-before-seen product set to hit store shelves in three months. This (and, of course, your cash compensation) can be found attached at the bottom of the box.

If any component of the promised package is missing or damaged, please contact the number below for a full refund."

She begins looking inside the box again, where she finds a roll of bills taped to the bottom. She unsticks it and unrolls the bills. She is left with five twenty dollar bills and a small gray plastic packet, unlabeled and unmarked.

The secret addition, she realizes, eagerly tearing the packet open. What is revealed is what looks to be a set of hand wipes. Her eyebrows raise at this.

Hand wipes? What the hell? Why are there hand wipes here?

She touches them, dry as a bone. She scoffs. *Great, they're not even GOOD hand wipes...* She places the products on the coffee table beside her and picks up the pamphlet again. *Maybe there's something in here*, she proposes.

After a bit of skimming, she finds the section about the "secret product," or as they call it, "Plastique Wipes," written in almost pretentiously fancy French terminology.

"To use Plastique Wipes, simply apply one of the wipes to your face and rub it across every available surface of your skin. In only a day, you should see miraculous results!"

Below, in much smaller print that requires a magnifying glass even to have a hope of reading, the article states:

"Warning: DO NOT, under ANY circumstances, use any other beauty care product after applying Plastique Wipes."

She sets the pamphlet on the couch beside her and looks again at the wipes. She picks one of them up again. Turning it over in her hands, she can't help but wonder if this is all a prank, a hoax, perhaps a method to hook her into getting an expensive as-all-hell subscription to Dollface or, at the very least, a ruse to rope her into some sort of contract.

There doesn't appear to be any such thing, though, and they *did* send the money. *Okay. Well, if this isn't a trick...* She picks up one of the wipes and begins wiping her face with it. Almost immediately, she jerks it back, wanting to throw it away. Dry as it is, the towelette feels more akin to sandpaper being rubbed on her skin. *The fuck?!* She screams to herself. *What the hell kind of beauty product is this? God, it's no wonder they haven't released it yet.*

Oddly enough, despite this, Rita still does as the instructions state, albeit painfully, and applies the wipe across her face. Once finished, she throws away the wipe and gets a cold rag to dab it with. As she walks from the kitchen back to the living room with the damp cloth, she thinks to look at herself in the mirror. She spots the mirror out of the corner of her left eye and hesitates.

There isn't any way whatever it is could've worked *this* quickly after applying. The pamphlet even stated that it took at least 24 hours to work. However, if nothing else, she feels that it may be necessary to check that she hasn't skinned her face to the bone the way it was feeling like she had. She turns to look, and surprisingly enough, there aren't any scabs, peeled skin, or anything resembling a carpet burn or anything of the sort.

Also, when Rita brings her hand up to touch her face, which is already looking at least a year or two younger than before, her skin feels buttery smooth. Holy mother of God. H-How is this possible? Her heart begins hammering. She could only barely recognize the woman, the burgeoning bombshell, staring back at her in the mirror—and this was only the beginning!

Elated, she snatches up her phone and, in two seconds, snaps no less than 200 selfies of her with her new look. Then, in a record-setting time of 10 minutes, she proceeds to blog said photos all across her FaceBook, Snapchat, Twitter, and Instagram stories. She can imagine the responses and all the undying praise people will shower her with. She giggles like a high school sophomore, thinking of all the random guys who'll hound her in her Private messages. In short, she feels like she did when she tried modeling back in high school.

God, I wish Ma could see me now. Take this, ya old hag. Tell me I can't get by with looks. She giggles again, eyeing the other beauty care products on her couch. *Maybe YOU couldn't, but that's because YOU didn't have Dollface back in the day, did you?*

As the day progresses, she feels she needs to do something she hasn't done in a long time. She calls her high school best friend, Janet, to invite her out for a manicure or maybe to the tanning salon. The call goes directly to voicemail.

"Hey Janie," she says in as nice a voice as she can muster, in spite of her frustration. I was wondering if you wanted to hit the town later today. Hit me back when you get this, 'kay? Love ya, sis. M'bye."

Hmph... The ONE time I try to get her to hang... Whatever, her loss. She then dashes to her room and begins throwing on her best outfit. She doesn't have many options when it comes to this sort of thing, which is part of the reason why she never takes Janet up on any of her offers to hit the town in the past. Eventually, though, she finds a cute tank top and a pair of jeans.

Throwing them on, she looks in the mirror again and smiles. With the sudden reformation of her face and the outfit, she now looks like she's 18 again, still a senior in High School. *Hell, I wish I could've looked this good back then.*

Grabbing her purse, she heads out of her house, gets in her car, and drives off for a day out on the town. She decides to turn her speakers on full-blast with her Spotify playlist, not giving a single damn in the world about whoever the hell would notice. It's here, though, that she notices something; she isn't wearing any makeup. She slams on the brakes in front of the red light.

How could she have been so careless? She *always* left the house with makeup on, even though all she's ever done outside her home is go to work. She almost panics but then remembers she always keeps a spare eyeliner and lip balm in her purse for cases such as this (or if what she is wearing somehow gets ruined).

She looks up, seeing the light is still red. She has about thirty seconds before it will change again. Hastily, she unscrews the cap of the lip balm and applies it as thoroughly as she can as the light turns green again. With her confidence and peace of mind restored, she hits the gas again and speeds the rest of the way into the downtown area and the strip mall.

While she steps out of her car, she begins to feel something burning on her lips. It's a slight feeling—nothing that's incredibly worrying. It's no worse than the sensation of hot liquid touching her lips or maybe a paper cut. She touches them, feeling nothing out of the ordinary, shrugs, and continues strutting happily into the mall. As she walks, people going in and coming out of the mall cast awe-filled glances at her. This makes a smirk of excitement and confidence cut across the corner of her lips. This causes the tingling from before to spike a bit, making the pain flare more than it already was.

She stops again, once again feeling her lips. Still, she finds nothing wrong with them, but now the discomfort is much more accentuated. Nevertheless, she shakes her head and continues walking. This was *her day*, damn it! Nothing was going to fuck this up for her.

She walks into the mall and immediately turns into a teenager again. She sprints up to the escalator and rushes into all the different department stores. The first on her list, obviously, was Victoria's Secret, then Lane Bryant, before hitting the perfume shops and shoe stores. With one hundred dollars to blow as she pleases, it's everything she can do not to run buck wild.

From new lipstick to go alongside the "emergency" one in her purse to new fragrant perfumes that make her smell like a flower, and even a couple of new, really nice, perhaps even sexy outfits, she couldn't be happier with her little excursion...except for the constantly flaring pain in her lips.

She's been ignoring it and still keeps a genuine smile despite it, but now it's becoming unbearable. What started as a mere tingling, perhaps tiny jabbing, now feels more like a ripping and tearing of her skin.

What the... What the hell is going on? Why does my mouth suddenly hurt so much?

She tries to shrug it off one last time by hitting the food court. She goes to her favorite vendor, the Chinese place, and orders a tray of orange chicken and fried rice. She gets her food and sits down, and as soon as she opens her mouth to take a bite, she screams. The worst agony she's ever felt shoots through her entire face. Everyone in the food court turns to look at her.

She jumps up from her table and makes a mad dash for the bathroom. Bolting in, she rushes to the mirror and picks frantically at her face. Now, amid her otherwise gorgeous face, Rita is horrified at the sight of her peeling lips. They are gray and flakey, and in some places, cracks can be seen, wide open and starting to bleed.

Her heart skips crazily in her chest. Her breathing becomes heavy, forming a lead brick in her lungs. What happened? Why are her lips now, all of a sudden, rotting?

She touched her lips, pinching and tugging at them, only to end up ripping them away from her face altogether. She screams from excruciating pain as well as horror. The rest of her face now burns in the same manner. Overcome with mania, Rita viciously claws at her face like a wild animal latched onto it.

With each swipe of her hands, each strike of her nails, more and more of her face tears away from her, until finally, she's completely unrecognizable as the young woman named Rita Johnson, with nothing left of her face but a reddish-pink, bloody mess of sinew and muscle. When another shopper rushes in, startled by her fit of screams, she too screams before running out and calling 911.

An ambulance arrives only five minutes later, but it's too little too late by this time. Rita lays motionless, her lifeless, skinless eyes staring up at the ceiling, forever frozen in perpetual horror.

"This just in: a local woman in JCPenny was found, just an hour ago, dead in the women's restroom with her face completely torn to shreds. Authorities are currently undecided on the possibility of foul play, though current reports suggest that her injuries were self-inflicted. It is unknown at this time how or why she might have done this to herself. More on the situation as it develops. Back to you, Jim."

Lindsey mutes the television. *Wow, the mall? That's what they're doing there now?* She scoffs, rolling her eyes.

Another ten minutes pass before she hears a knock at the door. She jumps up eagerly and answers the door to find a man holding a FedEx package she's been anticipating for the past four days. She snatches it and opens it inside, revealing a box containing the latest line of products from the ever-infamous beauty company, Dollface—and all for just $0.99.

God, I can't wait to try this all out. I can only imagine what the "mystery product" is.

MASTICATION

J uly 30th, 2022

Stream goes live at 3:00 p.m.

(Camera clicks on, subject's face takes center frame)

"Yo, what's up, guys? It's your boy, Melvin Masticator, here, and today, we're trying the titanic spread. And boy... I gotta say..." (Subject moves camera over to kitchen table) "I mean just *look* at all this, man!"

(Camera pans around table)

"Look at this: four deluxe salmon burgers *with bacon--* obviously, six large orders of fish sticks, two tuna melts, nine whole orders of fries, and to wash it all down..."

(Camera stops at four large drinks)

"Four titanic gulper Cokes!"

(Camera cuts back to subject's face)

"Now, the word on the street is, NO ONE has been able to eat all this food, all in under two hours, and live! Ooooh!" (Subject waves hands in front of camera)

(Images of headlines appear on screen with subject's voiceover)

"For those who don't know-- well, first of all, get outta the rock you live under-- but second, Rowboat Seafood Shack has been hosting their legendary Titanic challenge to see who can finish all this food here in under an hour and a half. Originally, that was all it was, a challenge, until…" (stock suspense sting plays in background) "…someone *DIED!*"

"Supposedly, there was only one who managed to pull it off. But he was found days later, dead. Rumors have spread that his body wasn't even recognizable afterward. Some say it was a deranged psycho sent from the restaurant to kill anyone who accomplishes the task. Others say it was something in the food. Most think it's high cholesterol. Who knows, though, right? Let me know what you guys think in the comments, and I'll read 'em later. But for now, I'm fuckin' *starving*, and this food's gonna go cold any second now, so let's eat."

(Camera cuts to subject sitting at table, surrounded by food)

"Alright, got my timer, hour and a half, let's go!"

(Subject begins eating food. At around the 1-minute mark on the timer, the subject stops and looks at the camera.)

"God, guys… I'm… I'm already feeling it, heh heh. Imma keep pushin', but I don't know…" (Subject chuckles and takes another bite)

(Subject continues eating. At around 3 minutes on timer, the subject puts sandwich down.)

"Mmm… Yeah, I gotta tell ya, heh heh…" (subject belches) "How many of you guys are gonna be mad at me if I can't finish this." (subject leans into camera) "Ah shit, you guys are really gonna make me eat all this?" (subject exchanges glances at food and camera)

(Subject picks up sandwich and takes bite. Timer is at 5:30 mark)

"Okay... I-It's... yep, it's definitely hitting me now." (subject starts clutching his stomach) "Okay, I really gotta go!" (subject gets up and runs away from camera)

(Subject remains off camera until timer hits 15 minute mark. Subject returns)

"Woo, sorry about that, guys. Had a little sitch there, but I'm back, and whoa... Jesus, I didn't even realize I was gone that long!" (subject begins shoveling food into his mouth. Subject begins speaking over mouthfuls of food)

"God... I'm so... HUNGRY!"

(Timer passes 20-minute mark. Half of the food is gone)

(Subject talks with mouth full) "So... so fuckin' hungry!"

(Subject continues shoveling food into his mouth until he cries out in pain after biting himself)

"The fuck?! I just bit my hand, heh heh. God, I'm still so fucking hungry though. I... I can't stop!" (Subject resumes shoveling food into his mouth until stopping again, crying out in pain again) "Fuck, I just bit myself again. God it hurts, too. I'm even bleeding, guys, look." (Subject shows left hand to camera, exposing large gash across the top of his hand) "I'm bleeding now, guys, and it hurts. A lot! But... But I can't stop! I... I have to... to..." (Subject crams sandwich in mouth)

(Subject devours the last of the meal with the timer reading 45:57)

"It's done, guys! The infamous Titanic spread is finished. And look," (Subject points to timer) "All in less than an hour!"

(Subject is seemingly out of breath, staring at camera wide-eyed)

"I... It's over... But... But I'm still so... So fucking..." (Subject's head starts wagging rapidly from side to side) "So fucking *hungry!*" (Subject's eyes dart wildly about the room before looking at his hands)

"So... So fucking hungry... I-I gotta keep going! I gotta have *more!*" (Subject holds up hands, staring intently at them) "So... *hungry!*"

(Subject proceeds to bite into his hand. In seconds, the subject's hand is stripped completely of flesh, and blood is spraying everywhere. A minute later, the subject falls to the floor, out of the camera's view. Stream continues.

Comments feed (56:03-1:12:07)

Erik_Reynolds56: "Yo... he good?"

JakNDak: "Bruh started tweakin', didn't he? XD

HannahStarr: "Guys... I don't think this is fake. Somebody needs to make sure he's okay."

G.Master: "Yo, You good @MattMasticator?

IanP. : "Y'all really falling for this shit? Bro's obviously faking it!"

HannahStarr: "I don't think so. He hasn't gotten up yet..."

Traci_16**: "You're right @HannahStarr. It's been almost ten minutes now..."

IanP. : "@HannahStarr, I'm telling you, he's fuckin' around here. Yo, Matt, quit playin' and get your ass up!"

HannahStarr: "He's still not getting up. Guys, I'm worried, I think we need to help him."

JakNDak: "How're we supposed to do that? Nobody here knows where he lives."

HannahStarr: "I'm gonna show this to the cops."

Traci_16**: "Good idea. I'll screencap the video for evidence if needed."

G.Master: "Me too."

IanP. : "Y'all are so damn gullible, but whatever, I guess."

Weeping Willow Ledger

August 4th, 2023

Local Foodie Found Eaten Alive?

By Triston Helms

"It was at around noon two days ago that the body of Matthew Ericks was found in his apartment, shredded. Authorities were supposedly given several anonymous tips, sourced from a live stream on YouTube, that Ericks had collapsed. Authorities claimed to have been "sickened to the worst degree," according to Officer Kent, when they found the young man's body completely missing his skin, with bits and pieces of it stuck in his teeth.

Authorities are at this time unsure as to the cause of this sudden cannibalism. Prevailing theories have suggested that it had something to do with the *Rowboat Seafood Shack's* "Titanic spread" meal, which has allegedly caused the death of at least two others in the last two years since its introduction. At this time, foul play has not entirely been ruled out. However, it won't likely be pursued as a possibility.

It must also be mentioned that all attempts to contact *Rowboat* regarding this and/or the other allegations against them and their product have failed.

ROOTED

The sun was glaring angrily into my eyes. Through my shades, I stared back into it, giving it the "fuck you too" grin it deserved. Yep, life felt good.

Just me, the tide, and the still-waking sun. Days like this were hard to come by. This was the first time in months I'd managed to get enough vacation time racked up to take a trip to the beach, not to mention all the other bills I ended up having to pay off-- repairs to my car after it got ran off the road by some jackass in a Chevy pickup, a hefty storage bill, and having to pay out a huge increase in this month's rent, thanks to the *one time* I let my friend bring her little poodle over, thinking my landlord wouldn't be *that* much of a prick with the whole "No Pets" rule, so long as it didn't mess anything up, right? Hell no!

But all that was behind me now. No, now it was just me and the beach. The mid-morning rays were starting to bear down on my skin. I lay back and let my body drink it all in. *That's it, Chrissy, you earned this.*

I can remember thinking I was actually rich for a moment. I visualized myself on the cover of Forbes or something like that, able to make money as a magazine model, sipping fancy cocktails while sunbathing like I did *every* day. Of course, I knew that wasn't likely ever in the cards for me, which was fine, but still... a girl *can* dream.

Being only mid-morning, next to fucking no one was out yet. I had the beach to myself, all nice and quiet. That is until I heard the sound for the first time.

It came from directly in front of me, from the shoreline. Now, understand, I'm no marine biologist or expert on sea life and/or what sounds they may or may not make, but I was pretty sure what I heard *wasn't* a fish. The closest thing I could think of, as far as relating it to a fish, that is, was maybe a humpback whale.

To paint a better picture here, imagine a whale's mating call mixing with the sound of a foghorn from a boat. That's what it sounded like. But, as far as I could see, there were neither whales nor boats anywhere in the ocean. There wasn't *anything* there, as a matter of fact. I sat up and leaned in for a closer look. Nothing.

Okay... So nothing's there, but then...

Looking closer, I noticed something else. The seagulls circling the ocean seconds ago were now darting away like their lives depended on it. I even caught a couple of them slapping each other with their wings, trying to force each other out of the way. My eyebrows raised at this.

What the hell is going on here? What's got them so worked up?

I looked at the water again. Still, there was nothing, although I started to see a small area in the middle where the water appeared to be rippling and not from the ocean's tide. These ripples were parting in a circular motion, like something or someone was coming out of the water. I stood up from my chair when I saw the waves fully part upward. The water exploded upward before crashing back down.

I ran up to the shoreline to get a closer look. I couldn't see where anything might've surfaced, and the water seemed to have spontaneously calmed itself. I stood for a good three to five minutes, wondering what the heck just happened, what that noise was, and trying to see what might've come out of the water. Finally, I shrugged and figured, "Eh, must've been a geyser or gas release from the ocean or something." Not a very plausible explanation, but again, how the hell would *I* know-- not an expert on the ocean and/or what goes on in it.

When I tried to turn around and return to my chair, I found my foot stuck to something. I looked down to see this dark greenish, wet *stuff* caked around my right foot. Maybe "caked" isn't the right word, though, more like planted. I say this because I went to lift the foot, and I shrieked in pain. I felt needles jabbing the top of my foot all at once. I stooped down to try and get the stuff off by hand. The second I touched any of them, though, it was over.

It was like my hand was a trigger for the stuff to sink deeper into my foot, putting me in much more unbearable pain—the same for when I tried one more time to jerk myself free. Insufferable pain, and the stuff would bury itself deeper.

So for about another minute and a half, I stood there, my foot aching like crazy, trying frantically to figure out how in the hell I was gonna find a way to get this shit off of me when, suddenly, it just fell off all on its own. I looked down, and there it was, the stuff, whatever the hell it was, looking all dried up and wilted like a pile of dead weeds. I looked down at my foot again and saw that, outside of a couple of tiny little spores where it'd been digging into my foot, I was pretty much unscathed. No blood, scars, nothing.

I couldn't feel any pain anymore, either. I knelt to touch the spores. It tickled a bit, but it didn't hurt or get irritated at all. *The fuck?*

I turned back and headed for my chair, dumbfounded. When I got back, I just decided to pack my stuff and return to the condo. The moment was gone, ruined by whatever that was. *Oh well. At least there's still another five days left in my vacation...*

I went back inside, and as I walked, I became drained. Every step started feeling more and more like I had to lift a 100 lb lead weight to do so. By the time I made it back to the condo, I was about ready to fall out the instant I turned the knob. In the end, I did end up falling face-first onto the couch. It wasn't a peaceful sleep, either. I hesitate to even call it "sleeping." It was more like I "shut down." I was unconscious, but when I woke up again, I felt like I hadn't slept in over three weeks.

It was somewhere around 10:30 or 10:45 pm when I woke up. My head was swimming, feeling like someone had gone and replaced it with a stack of bricks. Not even during my worst hangovers back in the day did I feel as bad a migraine as I felt that night when I woke up.

Then I realized something. I didn't know if it was the headache or something else, but I couldn't feel any part of my body. My arms and legs were both completely numb, completely disconnected from me. My body was basically dead weight, a pile of meat splayed out across my couch. No matter how hard I tried, how much I essentially screamed at my body to fucking move, it just wouldn't.

I laid there, miserable, trapped, and, worst of all, unable to fucking sleep. I couldn't take it anymore, so I managed to make myself roll over, falling face-first onto the floor. Then I noticed something alarming—my skin began crawling. I don't mean like out of any reaction or any sort of anything like that—no. I mean, my skin was *literally* crawling.

I watched bits and parts of the skin on the bridge of my nose start to sort of scurry up the length of it, traveling up to my head. It felt tingly, like something pricking me from the inside when this happened. My skin went pale soon following. I felt like my body was going cold, deathly cold, while I tried forcing my arms to move again so I could push myself up. It was pointless, though. So, feeling every bit as woozy and drained as I had hours before, I slowly slipped unconscious again.

The next time I woke up, I couldn't stop myself from screaming in absolute agony as soon as my eyes were opened. Imagine again that you just woke up, and something was coming out of you. I'm talking straight out of your stomach, a long, spiky sort of vine or tentacle maybe (as green as the thing was, it wouldn't have been hard to mix up the two, trust me), and it's *moving*, squirming around, snaking out of you and down to the floor. Can you imagine how that'd feel? If not, I understand. I know that's a rather colorful image, but I'll tell you what *I* did—I shrieked until my throat was damn near torn in half.

Here's the thing: as freaky as this all was (not to mention painful), that wasn't even the freakiest part. Out of the corner of my eye, I could see the vine/tentacle/thing coming out of my back, growing taller and taller, reaching up to the ceiling. When it did, I could also see a bunch of tiny little nubs or branches extending from it, reaching out to the walls of the condo.

Then, it started happening in other areas of my body. Large, dark green, wormy roots began painfully exploding out of me. First from the backs of my feet, then from my hips, then my arms themselves, before finally bursting from my stomach, punching straight through the floor and spreading all across everywhere else. From below me, I could hear mixed reactions of *"What in holy Hell?", "Oh my God, what IS that?",* and just straight up shrieking in panic.

All of this ended up, though, being more or less drowned out by my own ear-splitting howls of pain, which by this point was on the same level to me as having my arms slowly amputated, fully conscious, with an old, rusty hacksaw and then dumping a canister of salt over the profusely bleeding stubs. It was the equivalent of Hell on Earth, or so I thought, anyway.

That is until I found out just how much worse things would get when I felt something thick, heavy, and slimy worm up my throat. The three to five seconds it spent trying to burrow up and out through my trachea has to be, by far, the worst and longest three to five seconds of my entire life, bar none, even now. I couldn't breathe, and so I was dead sure that was going to be it for me. I wish it had been.

Though I did start seeing dark clouds hovering in the borders of my vision, I never passed out. I wouldn't be granted this mercy, and instead, I got to watch as the root or vine, the largest and thickest one to come out of me so far, erupted out of my mouth and split off into two different directions. One went for the window, while the other reached for the ceiling along with the others. The one that went for the window punched straight through it and slithered out into the wild.

It's been at least five and a half hours since that happened, and it's not showing any signs of stopping its growth and spread. I am trapped in my condo here, permanently attached to the floor, the building...hell, even the ground beneath me. I'm in the worst pain. I can't move, I can barely breathe, and I can't do anything to stop this.

I have no idea what this stuff is. But whatever it is and wherever it came from, I know this much: it definitely came from whatever the hell that shit on the beach was that'd latched onto my foot. I don't know just how many other people this stuff's affected already, though I can tell there are only very few, if really any, who might've made it out of the condo without being attacked and suffering the same way as me. If there are any out there, please know that I'm truly sorry and need your help.

Please, somebody, *anybody*; policeman, ambulance, firefighter...at this point, I won't argue with you calling a goddamn *landscaper* to come to the condo—just fucking *anybody* who can get rid of this thing! *Please!*

I don't have much time. I can feel it in my eye sockets now, all wriggly and slimy. Oh God, it's pushing out my fucking eyeball. It hurts so much.

Please, PLEASE God, help me...

I never wanted to be rooted to the beach, not like this!

HUNNYFRESH

I knew something was off the minute I looked in that fucking mirror. Call me crazy, but last I checked, "pimples" weren't supposed to be over six inches all around. Not usually, anyway.

Okay, okay, so I'd been using this new facial cream or whatever, right, called *Hunnyfresh*. It's, I think, supposed to be this new sort of face mask that uses a blend of tea leaves, oils from a laundry list of various exotic plants (you know, the kind you probably couldn't even pronounce right, no matter how fuckin' hard you try), and *supposedly* actual dew drops. The ads all said it was designed to tighten and smooth out your skin, sort of like Botox, only more "Eco-friendly" or whatever.

Obviously, as a forty-year-old mother of three, that was a big thing for me—trying to preserve my looks wasn't exactly easy for me. Hell, wrinkles had already started coming in at 37, and things haven't been exactly stress-free here at the Jameson house as of late. For one thing, I should mention that I'm a *single* mother of three. Daddy dearest ran off while I was giving birth to Brent, our youngest, to hook up with some cam-girl half his fuckin' age. He'd always been behind on his child support, which was basically always the story with him, although *this* month, he just flat-out said he wasn't going to pay up.

His ass in jail, sure, but that still doesn't help me, nor does the fact that I kept getting cut on my hours at work. Now top this shit sundae off with the fact that I've also had to take the car into the shop on four separate occasions this month alone, not even counting all the times before, and the fact that the kids are chomping at the bit for all these afterschool things they've been told about at school, and yeah, you now have a pretty accurate glimpse into the chaos that has been my life.

That was a mouthful, I know. I'm not looking for sympathy. I'm trying to emphasize that I spent four hundred dollars on a skincare product—and I think it's killing me.

So anyway, I'd been hearing about *Hunnyfresh* for at least the past three months. There were TV commercials, Facebook reels, and Instagram reels. People were showing them off on Snapchat and X. Obviously, I was a bit skeptical.

Yeah, their skin looked better, and yeah, it *supposedly* made people in their fifties or older look almost twenty-something again. Well, they did in the ads, anyway. I'm not stupid, though, and I know a damn filter job when I see one. I would know; I've done that myself (it was for an online dating profile I tried last year, and it didn't work out).

I'd all but written it off as a fraud until my friend Jackie came over with her son, Tommy, to play with my boys one Friday a few weeks ago. Now, understand that she's at least 45 or 46, and while she was never hideous, she didn't look young, either. That is, until she came over that day, looking like she had back in college when she was *literally* the hottest girl on campus. I remember how she laughed as soon as our eyes met as she saw how mine were about to shoot out like bullets at her from their sockets.

"Jesus, Jackie, how did you..." I remember trailing off, being at an utter loss for words.

She chuckled. "Here, Tom, why don't you and the boys go play while Mommy and Aunt Jameson talk for a bit?" she nudged her son. He was shy at first until Joel, Albert, and little Brent came rushing out of their rooms. Once the boys ran screaming into the back room, she and I sat on the couch.

"So, uh," I waved my hand over my face and added, "You gonna tell me about this?"

"Whitney, baby, I *know* you've heard of *Hunnyfresh* by now, haven't you?"

I remember scoffing. "You *actually* bought that?"

"Well, yeah," she said, almost patronizingly. "Question is, how come *you* haven't?"

I dodged this question by firing back with one of my own. "And all you've been doing is that? You've not been taking *any* other stuff with it?" She shook her head. "Nothing at all?"

"No, Whitney, I haven't taken nothin' except *Hunnyfresh* for the past four weeks now."

"How long have you had the stuff?"

"Four weeks."

My eyes grew. "Four weeks, and it does all this?" I waved my hand in front of my face again. She nodded excitedly.

"Yeah, and it doesn't require any doctor visits. Oh, and you think *I've* gotten younger because of it?" She rifled through her purse for a second before pulling out her phone. "You need to see my mother."

She turned the phone to face me. I damn near lost it. Sure enough, just like Jackie in front of me, she was almost unrecognizable. She was in her *sixties*, for Christ's sake. *Mid*-sixties, to be exact.

In the photo, you'd have sworn she was only pushing thirty. My breath was stripped from me. "H-How?"

"I'm tellin' you," she said, smiling, putting her phone back in her purse. "The stuff's the real deal."

"And there's no side effects? No itch, no sore spots, nothing?" She shook her head.

I leaned back on the couch. To say I was flabbergasted would've been a grievous understatement. I was *baffled!*

"Stuff's expensive, though," she said, snapping me out of my stupor.

"How bad?"

"Couple hundred. Three or four hundred, I believe."

My heart crashed right back down. "Three or four hundred? Yeah... maybe I won't after all..."

"But believe me, it's well worth the investment."

I wrinkled up my lip, contemplating if I *could* invest that kind of money into it. Clearly, the shit worked as advertised. Jackie was living proof. *But four hundred dollars?*

She slapped my lap and said, "You know what? I think you and I need to go to the mall tomorrow and get some for you."

I raised an eyebrow and chuckled. "What, that stuff makes you *act* like you're 20 again, too?"

She laughed and shrugged. "What can I say? Seriously, though, let's do it. You and me, tomorrow at noon." She stared excitedly at me, just like when we would dare each other to sneak out of our parent's houses to go to some party and get wasted back in the day.

I looked toward the back room. The boys' screams and hollers echoed down the hallway.

"So, you in?"

"I don't know, Jackie..." I looked back at her, biting my lip. "That's a lot of money."

"Well, let me ask you two questions then. First, how tired are you?"

I frowned.

"How much do you want to look pretty again, like you did in college?"

"You're saying I'm not pretty anymore?" I phrased this in a mock-offended tone.

She chuckled. "No, but age is catching up to you."

This time, my face kind of faltered—cheap shot.

"It's okay, though. It was the same with me, remember? That's what this stuff's for, isn't it?"

I sighed and told her she was right. Again, the stuff was apparently effective. "What was the other question?"

Her mischievous grin returned. "Who's your bestest friend in the whole wide world?"

I snickered and told her she was. She held up a gift card to Ulta for five hundred dollars.

This time, my eyes really did shoot out of their sockets. Well, okay, no, they didn't, not yet anyway. That would come later...after all the shit started.

She thrust the gift card in my hand and exclaimed, "Merry Christmas!" We sprang up and bearhugged each other, squealing like schoolgirls again.

We broke when we heard Joel's little voice crying, "What's wrong, mommy?"

Before I could say anything, Jackie piped up, "Mommy's excited for our little playdate tomorrow!" His eyes lit up.

"Playdate?!" he exclaimed. "Can I come?"

"This is for adults, honey," I told him.

"Oh." His head was just about to drop when one of the boys called out, compelling him to run back to the room.

"So, again, I ask... Are you in?"

"Hell yes!"

After that, we watched TV for about two hours before she said she and Tommy needed to head home. The following day, she texted me at 10:00 am, telling me she'd be there in about fifteen minutes. Noon was too long for her to wait, she told me. I took her side; the boys were at their grandmother's for the weekend.

She picked me up, and we headed over to Ulta. There, she led me by the hand to the *Hunnyfresh* wall. It was their largest wall and the most populated. Trying to wade our way through that crowd gave me flashbacks to times when I'd be brave and stupid enough to try shopping on Black Friday.

Once we managed to get to the wall—alive—she showed me all of the different Hunnyfresh products. I would've been amazed at the selection. Hell, I'd have likely spent half the day just trying to search the wall, looking at all of the different products, if the crowd wasn't trying every second to shove me and her out of the way.

I asked her if she could find me the same kind she used. She guided me over to it, and we swiped it up as fast as we could. It was the last one.

We paid for it, a couple of perfumes, and some nail polish before heading out. We grabbed a bite to eat at the pizza joint across the street. While we were eating, Jackie was scrolling through her phone while I was looking at my new beauty mask. I turned it around in my hands, examining it for any warning labels or anything.

Just like Jackie had said, there were none. Everything looked exactly like it should. I popped the lid a bit and took a whiff. It smelled like the Earle Grey tea with honey I make every morning. God, I couldn't wait to get home and try it on.

"How long did you say it took before you started getting results again?" I asked her.

"Well, to look like this," she waved her hands across her face, "it will take about four weeks. But you'll see improvement after the first week, I promise. Just use it before you go to bed every day, just like any other face mask."

After lunch, she drove me home.

That night, just like she told me, I applied the *Hunnyfresh* right after putting the boys to bed. I went to sleep believing I'd wake up the next morning as the sexiest bitch alive (something me and Jackie, along with a few of our other friends, would say to each other to psych ourselves out).

The process repeated the rest of the week, and again, just like Jackie had said, the stuff was having an effect. Already, I could look in the mirror, and most of my wrinkles had smoothed out. I looked five years younger. A couple of times throughout the week, Joel or Albert would come up to me and ask me who I was and what I did with their mommy—it made me giggle.

It was about the Wednesday of week 3 when I decided to apply a little more—*maybe* another fingertip-full—each night. Again, there were no warnings against it. At first, everything seemed normal. Granted, I don't think there were any improvements, but there weren't any side effects either.

That was, until just this past Monday. I woke up that morning with a nasty itch. I felt like I'd been damn near clawing my face off before I could even get out of the bed. I got up and went to the bathroom to find my face littered with zits. Not the normal tiny ones you'd just pop between your fingernails. No, these were about the size of my thumb, and they were all over my face.

At first, I thought maybe I'd contracted chicken pox or something. I didn't feel anything else associated with that, though, so I went for some concealer cream. Since the biggest problem was the itch, I figured a little antibiotic ointment and some concealer would do the trick until it went away. I quickly found that to be the worst thing I could've done.

As soon as I put the concealer on my skin, the shit burned like I'd put acid on it. I tried scrubbing it back off, which caused it to burst. Then, the *real* pain began.

Another thing that set whatever was on my face apart from zits or pimples was the fact that, instead of pus dripping out of the pustule, it was this dark black gunk that burned like tar as it ran down my face in streams. Every second it spent on my skin was agony, searing and reddening. Before too much longer, my head looked like a fire alarm, glowing with how enflamed it all had become.

I was about to wipe it all off when one eye went dark. I tried blinking, but that did me no good, so I put my hands up to my face, only to realize there was nothing in my left eye socket. When I looked down into the sink, there it was—my eyeball…completely dislodged, sitting next to the drain.

Panicking, I tried to pick it up, only to knock it into the drain. There was no stopper, either, so it ended up falling right down the pipe. That was the moment I couldn't hold it in any longer, and I screamed. Two seconds after I did that, my tongue ejected out of my mouth, landing in the sink where my eyeball had just been.

My stomach turned over after that, and before I could even turn to hurl into the commode, I spat my guts up right there in the sink. Everything was a liquidy red, and it burned my throat and chest coming up. While I was vomiting, my remaining eye tried to come loose, too. I managed to keep it pushed in, but about three-fourths of my teeth came out with the rest of the fluids.

In my commotion, I'd woken up Albert, who came running into my room. He got one good look at me, spewing bloody muck all over my bathroom, and he took off screaming. About five seconds later, I heard him shouting at someone to send an ambulance because Mommy was very sick. Thank God I'd taught him how to use the phone for emergencies.

It was about ten minutes later when they arrived. By that time, I'd lost all the strength in my legs to stand, and I was on my side, still spurting the red stuff in choked gulps. They rushed me to the ER, where I've been ever since.

It's been a pain in the ass to try and type all of this with my phone. The nurses gave it to me so I could communicate with them through texts since I couldn't talk anymore. The boys have been with my mother for the past two weeks now. My fingers feel like they'll be the next to fall off.

The nurses have told me they haven't been able to find the cause of any of this. I told them about the *Hunnyfresh*, of course. They said they'd look into it, but they'd never dealt with any other cases like mine because of *Hunnyfresh*, so it was unlikely that it was the cause. I don't know. I don't know if I'll even get out of here alive.

Every five minutes, my eye keeps trying to pop loose, so I have to push it back in. My jaw feels like the bones are disconnecting at the joints. I can't eat or drink anything, so I've been hooked into at least seven I.V. machines the entire time.

I'm scared. I don't want to die here. What am I supposed to do?

WALKING SKIN

As if there haven't been enough problems with Daniel's day thus far, here's another one. On his screen, the alarm notifications for sector 6 of the facility are screaming at him. It has been this way for over three and a half minutes. Long enough now that, if this were a red-level emergency—say, a leak or containment breach—it's wraps for him and every underpaid desk monkey in that godforsaken place. Protocol mandates that the evacuation call be announced no later than two minutes following the initial notification (and really, they'd STRONGLY urge you to have that done within the first minute-and-a-half mark).

The problem is, Dan's had a really rough one as of late. Between dealing with Hannah failing in two of her honors classes, as well as getting into a fistfight with two of the other girls on her school's cheerleading squad, and Pamela constantly screaming at him over the fact that he's never around the house to do his part—which apparently means being the one to do *all* the cleaning of *everything* and still make over six figures (He tries to make her happy, but is it enough? No.), he hasn't seen a decent night's sleep in over three days. And on all the days for there to be a situation like this at the facility, it has to be after last night's little falling out that just narrowly avoided domestic violence charges on both of their parts.

The alarm blasts into his ears, carrying on into his dream. In his dream, the noise blends with the music of the trancelike nightclub EDM beats, surrounded by hundreds of hot babes, all of them rubbing against him with their slender, scantily clad bodies, moving around in a snakelike weaving motion, with their hands moving up and down their bodies and his and...

"Burkes!" shouts Greg, the head of the facility's science division.

Daniel's head jerks up so quickly that it's an honest surprise he didn't give himself whiplash.

"Burkes, what's going on? Why haven't you signaled an evac yet?!"

Bewildered and probably a good deal spooked, Daniel starts throwing his head in every direction. His heart stops when he sees the monitor flashing, and his jaw falls to the floor.

"Move!" shouts Greg as he shoves him to the side and mashes the intercom button. "Attention all staff in the East wing of the facility! This is a Red-level emergency! There has been a containment breach in hall seven, and a possible biohazard has been released. Please exit immediately through the emergency exits located in hall three. DO NOT USE ANY OF THE ENTRANCES FROM HALL ONE TO SIX!"

The entire time Greg speaks, Daniel's heart remains dead in his chest. *Biohazard release?!*

For ten years, he's worked as a safety monitor for Monolith Site 46D, and at no point during this time has there ever been anything close to this. The closest real "emergency" was the one time a small chemical spill leaked out past one of the chem labs, and even *that* was a yellow level at best—nothing that would have warranted a mass evacuation like this. "What is it?" asks Daniel.

Greg turns and gives him a look he's only seen on the faces of war survivors. "I... I don't know..." Greg wipes his face roughly with his palms and sighs. "I don't know, Burkes... but whatever it is, if we don't get the..." He pauses.

Daniel sees the toll it's taking on him to breathe—like he's been running at full speed in a triathlon or something. Given the circumstances, he probably had been running into the office. "Greg?" he asks.

Daniel moves closer to try to keep him from possibly passing out. Greg raises a hand to stop him, shooting him a look that says, "I'm fine," before clutching his stomach. He doubles over and spews up what looks like a mix of cherry Kool-aid and bleach.

Daniel leaps back to avoid getting splashed by any of it, a reflex that likely saves his life, with the way the stuff begins eating through the floor on contact. Greg's eyes are bulging as this happens. Soon, crimson streams begin gushing from the poor bastard's eyes, and he collapses onto his face. Acidic red bile continues pouring from his mouth, and Daniel sees the light fade rapidly from his eyes. Then, the rest of his body goes completely still.

Daniel turns and runs out through the exit. He sprints through the main corridor and out into the passageway connecting halls three and four, burning through just about every reserve of energy he has. He doesn't look back, either, not that there is any reason to in the first place. His pursuer isn't some maniac but a pathogen.

He stops then, just outside of hall four. All around him, the area is quiet. The halls, dark and still, indicate no sign of life. His mouth opens, readying to call out to see if someone, *anyone,* can hear him and is still alive. Then he hesitates. Down at the far end of the hall behind him, hall five, a loud yet strained moaning sound echoes off the steel walls. His head snaps back to see what can make such a noise. He is met, however, with nothing but a pitch-black hallway.

His knees are quivering, threatening to buckle at any second. Daniel takes a step back from the hallway when another tortured moan rings out from the hallway. Then, the painful moaning becomes an agonized shriek, and

Daniel's heart stops. Following this is a series of shrieks and howls of agony mixed with the sound of something tearing like paper, only with a wet sort of squelching noise accompanying it. Then, the halls become quiet again. Daniel stands, shaking, every muscle and nerve telling him to move—to investigate or flee.

Of the two, Daniel chooses the former. He takes a minute, *heavily* measured step toward the hallway. As he does, another wet, squelchy sound echoes off the walls. A silhouette appears from the room dead ahead, resembling a person slumped over or slouched. The figure stands there for a second, making no movements until Daniel falls back. Then, as if flipping a switch, the figure jumps into action, staggering forward. As it does, its body appears to fold backward in a manner indicating it has no spine.

Daniel, nonetheless, staggers back at the sight. One of his steps rolls over on the side of his ankle, and he falls straight on his ass. This prompts the figure to transition from a shambling trod out of the hallway to a full-on sprint. Before Daniel can even try to crabwalk away, the thing is on top of him. His heart freezes for a second time.

The figure appears to be one of the lab workers—Dr. Judith Renshaw, according to her name tag. If she weren't wearing it, he wouldn't recognize her. He works in the central office, while she's a so-called "Lab monkey." He has no idea why she's in this area or what she was doing moments ago. It's just another indication that he has no clue what he's up against. Even *if* he knew her, it's entirely possible he still wouldn't recognize her, as it resembles her *only* in the sense that it's her skin.

Whatever this thing is, one thing is certain: it *isn't* Dr. Renshaw. It isn't human, either. It wears the skin of Dr. Renshaw, but that's it.

She leers at Daniel. Helpless to flee or fight, he stares back into the thing's sagging, gnarled, gory, empty eye sockets. Looking closer, Daniel notices there don't seem to be any bones under the skin. The thing is an animated pelt of wrinkly, sagging flesh.

The lower jaw of this creature distends, sagging down limply while seizing Daniel by the shoulders. Despite the absence of muscles or bones, she still has the grip of an orangutan; from the looks of it, she's about to rip him apart like one. He struggles but cannot move a muscle. The creature emits an ear-splitting screech that Daniel can't shield his ears from.

Daniel closes his eyes, waiting for the creature to make its move and end him. About a minute goes by, and he realizes he's okay. He's still in the creature's grasp when he opens his eyes. The creature continues staring him down, cocking its head from one side to another, admiring him or finding something curious about him.

From behind, a loud groan comes from the hallway. He darts a side glance over his shoulder to see more fleshy pelts stumbling out of the darkness. His heart races again, and he begins squirming in the creature's hands to no avail. The creatures from the darkness draw closer, surrounding him. They gather, and one from the crowd sticks out to Daniel—Greg, or at least his husk. Daniel's eyes double in horror while they close the gap.

"No! No! God, please, no! Get away from m—"

His words are cut short when one of the pelt-creatures grabs his hair from behind and yanks his head back. Another then forces their fleshy hands at his jaws, forcing them apart. As this happens, Daniel tears his throat to shreds, screaming until another creature comes and silences him by breathing a cloud of red vapor into his face. His screaming instantly morphs into desperate wheezing. The cloud dissipates, settling into Daniel's lungs, and the creatures release him and back away, leaving him to writhe in agony.

His body spasms to a degree that each convulsion is painful. His vision fades, and darkness engulfs the entire world around him. His head pounds and his body becomes cold. His chest aches from some immense pressure as if a lead weight had been dropped on it. His skin starts to feel thin, like he can feel it peeling away layer by layer. The dark clouds in his eyes start watering, with his eyeballs slowly melting into slag. The same is happening with his organs as they slowly spill from every orifice of his body.

Eventually, the pressure builds so much that his body arches upward in a major spasm, resulting in the sound of tearing bouncing across the room's walls. One last horrified wail of agony, and the lights finally go out for Daniel for good.

"This just in: the site of acclaimed science division Monolith has just released a warning of the outbreak of a highly dangerous biohazard. We have Rhonda Pike on the scene, Rhonda?"

"That's right, Jim. I am standing outside Monolith site 46D, where lockdown procedures have been implemented. Around me are two SWAT teams and one of the site's cleanup crews. We are unaware of any specifics regarding what happened or what the supposed biohazard is. Still, we are told that the initial lockdown was triggered by a Red-level emergency, indicating a breach of containment regarding a biohazardous chemical.

"Authorities have mandated that all residents within ten miles are to evacuate and seek shelter until otherwise notified. If you look over here, you'll see one of the officer—

"Wait a minute... Tom, zoom in. Right there, zoom in. Is that one of the officers?

"One of the officers is coming this way. Let's see what he has to.... Wait a minute...

"Oh God, it's coming for us! Tom, get in the van an—AUGGHHH!"

"Rhoda?! Rhonda, are you there? Okay, uh... Cut! Cut to commercial, back in fifteen...

"Dear Christ..."

AFTERPARTY

R ick knew it was going to be a shit day when he woke up on the floor—*again*! *Knew I shouldn't have thrown that damn party last night,* he thought to himself as soon as his eyes opened. Nothing good ever came of them by morning.

He didn't expect that he wouldn't be able to get off the floor.

He tried to sit up, only for half of his face to suction itself to the carpeting. He pushed against the ground as much as he could, only to find that his hands were also stuck.

Damn it, Kendall. I swear, one of these days, I'm gonna get you for your little pranks. "Ha ha, good one, Kendall," he shouted. "The old glue trick again. Glad to see you've not developed any new tricks since last ye—"

When he attempted to lift his hand, his breath caught in his throat. Straining to lift himself barely an inch off the ground, Rick saw a white, silky film connecting his palms to the floor.

The hell, this isn't glue.

His eyes doubled in size while his stomach turned over. In one fluid jerk, he ripped his body up off the ground—which hurt like hell—and ran to the bathroom, emptying his stomach into the commode. The whole time, all he could think was, *how in the hell did I wake up stuck to the floor with jizz?!* When his head lifted, and he got a good look at the blood-red and black substance now smeared all over the bowl, the question *very* quickly became, *what the hell is this in the toilet?!*

Before he could process any of this, his stomach sent shockwaves into his chest. Thick and extremely hot bile rose from his throat, and he was right back, hunched over the toilet, choking up more of the stuff. He was heaving, having to push it all out, almost as if he were trying to spew up a pile of rocks.

This time, the bile was acidic, tearing his esophagus open with each second he spent forcing it out. It didn't take him long now to realize he might be in serious trouble.

What the fuck did I drink last night?!

He scrambled for his phone, only to drop it, shattering it upon impact, while more corrosive bile rose from his stomach. It flowed more freely this time, though it still burned like hell. He stayed, emptying every last drop of his stomach until he started to lose consciousness.

His heart echoed in his ears. His head pounded, battering his brain around inside his skull. His head felt light, making him feel like he had no muscle and that his skin was draped like curtains over his bones. Eventually, consciousness faded completely, and the last thing he saw was the rim of the toilet before it connected with the brow of his right eye, bouncing his head off of the toilet onto the floor.

Whether because of the panic, the nausea, or the head trauma, Rick was knocked out *cold*.

When he woke up about half an hour later, one of the first thoughts to cross his dazed mind was, *Holy shit, I'm still alive (Right?).* His eyesight was slow to recompose, but he didn't need to see to realize shit still wasn't all good. No, he figured this out about five seconds after he woke up again and realized that, once again, his head and hands were stuck to the floor.

When he tried to move his arms and legs, they felt like they'd lost all the muscle and ligaments with that last episode over the commode. He had no strength and, frankly, no will even to try and fight to stand up again. He wasn't in pain or panic. More than anything, he was just exhausted. It was the feeling you'd expect to have after having your entire large intestine emptied in a single hour: drained, dizzy, and numb, with your stomach shooting bullets of stabbing pains throughout your whole body that make you curl into a ball.

That is until he caught sight of what happened when he gave one last jerk to try and pry his hand off the ground. His eyes shot from their sockets—almost literally, believe it or not—when he saw his hand had been degloved. The flesh now rested in a bloody heap on the floor only half a foot from his face.

Strangely, though, it wasn't even this alone that horrified him. Instead, it was the fact that replacing his normal muscle tissue underneath was an alien, sharp, piercing sort of appendage with about a million microscopic hairs protruding from it. The hairs on it twitched wildly, swaying and twirling in their disgusting follicles.

What the... The fuck is this?!

He cried out in agony again, feeling something forcing its way up his throat again. *Oh God, no, no more, PLEASE,* he thought. His eyes darted to the landline telephone Kendall's boomer parents kept (*"Thank you, boomers!"*).

It's my only chance!

Using his foreign appendage, he dragged himself along the floor as quickly as possible, which is to say just above a snail's pace but still slower than a slug. The closer he got to the phone, the more of his skin was stripped away, sticking to and leaving a trail of blood and gore along the flooring. With each bit stripped away, more of an insectoid body was revealed beneath Rick's skin.

Rick's sight blurred again. He couldn't fade out now—not yet. He would be a goner if he did.

The tightness in his throat finally erupted from his mouth, revealing not the corrosive bile from before but a new set of twin jaw-like pincers, which punched out through his mouth. As horrific as this was, he did his absolute damnedest to ignore it and keep pulling himself along. When he finally made it to the table with the phone, the only part of him that resembled a human being was his face—minus, of course, the pincers.

The rest of his body had become that of a gigantic black widow. By now, the phone was, to him, nothing but a blurry dot on the table.

Still, he reached for it, only to knock it over with his arachnid appendages. He continued scrambling for it, but no matter what, all he could do was knock the receiver around like a hockey puck. Eventually, his eyesight shut off completely, and with it, his rational mind. His last thought—his very last fleeting thought that was soon devoured by the darkness and fog of his new animal mind was, *What the fuck did I drink at that party?!*"

WEIGHT LOSS

The following is a string of texts between me and my best friend, Craig. He was found a week ago, half drained of blood with his stomach split open. There was no sign of foul play (or so the detectives wanna claim anyway. The investigation's supposedly "ongoing," but frankly, I think there's something else to it, something they don't want anyone to know about. For reference to what I'm talking about, here's everything I have.

<u>Monday</u>

<u>(3:45 A.M.)</u>

-- "Yo, U up man?"

-- "I am NOW."

-- "Shit, sry man..."

-- "Sure ya are..."

-- "Look. is it important?"

-- "Duh. U rly thnk Id wake Ur ass up if it wasn't?"

-- "Bro... I LITERALLY have snapshots of you blowing my phone up at ONE IN THE MORNING, just to talk about your latest molly trip, don't try me with this shit."

-- "Come on, dude, Ur STILL on about that? Look I said I was sry, ok? Jesus, I gotta lick ur fuckin feet to get U off my back?

-- "Nah, that's what I got ur girl 4. ;)"

-- "Fuck you. XD"

-- "Like I said, what I got ur girl 4. Anyway though, seriously, what's up?"

-- "Ok, so U know how I've been tryin to get ripped right?"

-- "Yeah, I think I remember U sayin' somethin' about that, why?"

-- "Well, I was actually about to give up, you know?"

-- "HA! I knew it!"

-- "I knew ur fat ass couldn't stay off the honey buns! XD"

-- "Hey, fuck U, Ive actually been off that shit for the past three weeks and hell, ALL I HAVE been eating is damn celery sticks."

-- "Felt like a damn rabbit."

-- "Been hittin the gym 2. 3 times a week. I'll have U know I've also been lifting better than 280."

-- "Shit dude. That's like, 2 mes. Maybe even 2 & a half. Nice."

-- Yeah, so U better watch out how U talk about my girl. >;)"

-- "Anyway, seriously tho, I felt like I hadn't been seein any gains, so I was about 2 quit, right?"

-- "Well, then I found this late last night."

-- (Craig shared a link)

-- "Whut the fuck?"

-- "Cool, right?"

-- "Bro, R U sure U ain't having another 1 of ur little trips again here?"

-- "No, why?"

-- "Read this shit again and U tell ME why."

-- "Bro, seriously, this is talking about a fucking PARASITE being injected into U, man.

-- "U RLY wanna walk around w/ a fuckin critter inside U?"

-- "Bruh, chill."

-- "It ain't a Parasite- says so on the page, which you'd know if U ACTUALLY read it."

-- "It's a bacterial microorganism that eats fat cells. U poop em out when they're done doing their thing."

-- "No harm to the person."

-- "Okay, first off, yeah, I DID actually read the form, and I noticed something that WASN'T there."

-- "Like what?"

-- "Oh, I don't know, maybe TEST RESULTS!"

-- "And?"

-- "AND"?! What do you mean, "And?" For fuck's sake, you don't AT ALL care about the fact that this thing, whatever the fuck it is, hasn't even been fucking tested yet?!"

-- "Like, what if this thing is some sort of bioweapon from the government or something? Ever thought of that?"

-- "U missed the best part then. They're paying for volunteers."

-- "So wait, U want to sign up for something like this, and U don't even know if it's safe, just 4 some $?!"

-- "Dude, the fuck?"

-- "Aren't U the one always saying life's all about taking risks?"

-- "Yeah, but I also tell U to B smart about it, don't I?"

-- "Look, U want 2 do this, fine. I can't stop U, alright."

-- "Just... PLEASE, if U do decide 2 do this, be smart about it."

-- "Do some research."

-- "Find out just what the hell's in this thing."

-- "Promise me you'll do that, 4 me @ least?"

-- "Fucking hell, fine "DAD" I'll "Do more research."

-- "Seriously man, U worry 2 damn much sometimes."

-- "Sorry I care about my bro?"

-- "I mean, look, I just don't wanna see ur ass on the news next time I turn my TV on, looking like the thing from "Alien" just crawled out of ya or something freaky like that."

  -- "Yeah, ok..."

  -- "I get it."

  -- "I rly do wanna do this, though."

  -- "But I'll try looking a little more into it, if it'll make you sleep easier."

  -- "It'll definitely help."

  -- "Look, I gotta be @ work in a couple hours. I'll talk 2 U sometime later."

  -- "In the meantime, DON'T DO ANYTHING STUPID!"

  -- "Jesus Christ, I said I'd hold off & look more into it, didn't I?"

  -- "I'll prolly holler @ U sometime later on tonight, What time U out?"

  -- "Not till 10."

  -- "Gotta pull another double..."

  -- "FUCK me."

  -- "Thought that was what my girl was 4 ;)"

  -- "Shut up. XD"

  -- "Anyway, night dude."

  -- "Night."

<u>Web Page from link (paraphrased)</u>

(Note: The link was not specific regarding any corporation or anything regarding who was funding it or conducting these experiments. I've tried searching for answers but haven't found anything, and when I went to look for the actual page again after hearing what happened to Craig, it was removed.)

<u>Attention!</u>

Are you tired of breaking yourself with constant exercise, only to garner <u>NO RESULTS</u>?! Then stop everything you're doing and read through, as this offer is extremely limited in its availability and on a first-come, first-serve basis.

For years, men and women all across the globe have been trying to crack the ancient secret regarding weight loss. It's something we all strive tirelessly for—to look good, no matter what size your britches are, to rock that swimsuit, and to generally feel good about looking at yourself in the mirror, right? Thing is, it's something so few have been able to ACTUALLY achieve without the use of drugs or supplements that, let's face it, cause more problems than they solve, yes?

Well, that's where we come in.

That's right. Our team of expert physicians has worked just as tirelessly as you to discover the secret to lasting weight loss, and now, we're proud to announce that we've hit a breakthrough! After YEARS of research, we've finally found what we are confident is the one and only true solution to not only shedding that bloat but also keeping it off.

Using a micro-organic bacteria, we've found something that effectively eats away the adipose tissue in all areas of your body. The best part is, as it is merely a bacteria, once it's done, usually taking only about 2-3 days, it gets flushed right down the porcelain express along with the rest of the waste. Yep, in and out in only 3 days! Then you get to look like a movie star!

For a limited time only, we are offering the first 100 people the sole privilege of having this secret revealed to them FREE! Yes, we said it, absolutely FREE, and that's not all. We're not only offering this once-in-a-lifetime opportunity at no cost to you-- AT ALL-- but we're also offering a handsome sum of no less than $5,000 compensation, as well as double that in collateral damage, should unforeseen effects or circumstances occur (which it won't). That's how confident we are that you'll be able to see a miracle happen with this!

So call today at (XXX) XXX - XXXX and reserve your spot to take part in this!

<u>Tuesday</u>

<u>(1:15 P.M.)</u>

-- "Yo, so I thought about it…"

-- "Imma do it."

-- "U sure, dude?"

-- "Yeah."

-- "K, well, have U looked into it anymore?"

-- "U even know what this "Micro organism" is?"

-- "Well no. Not entirely."

-- "?"

-- "I thought U said U weren't gonna do this without doing research first."

-- "I have."

-- "See, I started looking online for it."

-- "Wasn't much, but I think I found something like whatever it is they're using."

-- "And?"

-- "So check it."

-- (Craig has shared a link)

-- "From what I'm seeing here, it looks like this thing's something called "*Bifidobacteria*". Apparently, it's been used on rats before & worked. Says it could even decrease the fat without decreasing energy."

-- "Ok, but how do U know this is the same thing?"

-- "Like I said, I don't yet."

-- "But dude, I'm telling U, I feel like this's legit."

-- "Bro…"

-- "Look, I get it, U rly wanna lose weight, but… I RLY don't think U should do this."

-- "There's too much we don't know & it scares me that there's nothing about it on the site other than "microorganism"."

-- "Just please…"

-- "Trust me on this, ok?"

-- "Please?"

-- "Whatever man."

-- "I can't stop U."

<u>Wednesday</u>
<u>(2:30 P.M.)</u>

-- "Yo, I just got out."

-- "Oh yeah?"

-- "So how'd it go?"

-- "U feel any different?"

-- "Any side FX?"

-- "Nah man, I feel great!"

-- "Actually no, I feel better than great."

-- "I feel fuckin' AMAZING!"

-- (Craig sent a photo)

-- "Holy shit, dude!"

-- "That/s U?!"

-- "Damn str8! ;)"

-- "Good God, U look a hundred pounds lighter!"

-- "I know, right?"

-- "So what all did they do?"

-- "They suck ur intestines through a silly straw or something?"

-- "XD"

-- "Nah man, they gave me a shot in the arm (which hurt like a MUTHAFUCKA, btw), and in like, 10 min., maybe 15, I looked in the mirror and well..."

-- "So they injected U with the bacteria?"

-- "Yeah."

-- "Any chance they told U what it was called?"

-- "Nah man, they wouldn't tell me."

-- "U didn't ask, did U?"

-- "Actually, yeah, I did."

-- "And they still wouldn't tell U?"

-- "Nuh-uh."

-- "Hm..."

-- "That doesn't sound safe, dude."

-- "Ngl, this sounds like something other than a trial 4 weight loss."

-- "Bro, can U PLEASE chill the fuck out? I'm fine, I just told U that."

-- "Aight, aight, U win."

-- "They at least give U the money?"

-- "Yeah, why?"

-- "Nothing, just wondered, you know, since they won't tell U what ur actually getting into."

-- "Bro, I'm pretty sure they just don't want the world knowing about it before they're ready 2 release it, U know?"

-- "Kinda like how movie companies don't want spoilers leaking before release day."

-- "Ok, but movie companies don't usually gamble on people's health like this either."

-- "Especially not without at least telling them what the fuck it is they're actually getting into."

-- "Well, bottom line is, I'M FINE!"

-- "U can rest easy now, ok?"

-- "Yeah sure, whatever."

-- "Just..."

-- "What?"

-- "If U find urself feeling weird, AT ALL, please call me, ok?"

-- "Ok."

-- "I'm serious about this, Craig."

-- "I promise U"

-- "Anything starts feeling fucky at all, U will B the 1st person I call."

-- "I swear on my momma about that."

-- "Not helpful, dude."

-- "Ur mom's dead"

-- "OF STOMACH CANCER!"

-- "Shit, that is right..."

-- "My bad, but U get my point tho."

-- "Yeah..."

-- "Aight, well I gotta go."

-- "Rhonda's blowing my phone up."

-- "Wanna hang tomorrow?"

-- "Sure, I'm out @ 3 tomorrow."

-- "Awesome, we'll hang for a bit @ Wing Station."

-- "Christ dude, U JUST got all that weight off & ur already trying 2 get it all back?"

-- "XD"

-- "Fuck U 2."

-- "Don't make me say it >;)"

-- "XD"

-- "Later bro."

-- "L8er."

Wednesday

(5:45 P.M.)

(Rhonda's number)

-- "Hey uh, Liam..."

-- "Rhonda?"

-- "Hey sweetheart, what's up?"

-- "When's the last time U heard from Craig?"

-- "Um... Like a couple hours ago, why?"

-- "He said U & him were gonna hang."

-- "Yeah, I mean, we were supposed 2."

-- "I haven't seen him tho..."

-- "Really?"

-- "Weird, ain't like him to ignore txts."

-- "Especially not from U."

-- "Well he was supposed to come by my house @ 3:30, but he never showed."

-- "I've already tried txting & calling him, but no luck with either."

-- "Damn..."

-- "Yeah... so can U like, help me out?"

-- "See if U can get in touch with him."

-- "Aight, give me a sec."

<u>Wednesday</u>

<u>(6:12 P.M.)</u>

<u>(Craig's number)</u>

-- "Hey man."

-- "Where U @?"

-- "Rhonda's been trying 2 call U."

<u>Wednesday</u>

<u>(6:25 P.M.)</u>

<u>(Rhonda's number)</u>

-- "U heard anything back from him yet?"

-- "Nope."

-- "U asked him yet?"

-- "Yeah."

-- "When?"

-- "Like, 10 min. Ago."

-- "& STILL nothing?"

-- "I'm sorry..."

-- "Can U call him?"

-- "Maybe he's got it on "Do not disturb" or something."

-- "Not likely."

-- "Plus I just tried about 3 min. Ago."

-- "Str8 2 voicemail."

-- "Oh my God…"

-- "Liam… What if something's happened 2 him?"

-- "Calm down, what do U mean?"

-- "Well, He told U about that thing @ the clinic, right?"

-- "Yeah."

-- "Told him it wasn't a good idea."

-- "Far be it from me to get him 2 listen 2 me tho."

-- "I know, right?"

-- "I told him the same thing!"

-- "Rhonda, let me ask U something."

-- "U spoke 2 him on the phone earlier today, right?"

-- "Yeah, he told me we'd hang out today, why?"

-- "He say anything 2 U about feeling any type of way?"

-- "Huh-uh."

-- "U sure?"

-- "No."

-- "I mean… I don't think so."

-- "?"

-- "What do U mean?"

-- "I need U 2 not bullshit me on this."

-- "What did he say 2 U exactly?"

-- "Well, he told me his stomach was feeling weird after he ate a leftover chili dog from the fridge."

-- "What else?"

-- "He said he felt like something was pushing itself out of his stomach."

-- "But he said he'd be fine after using the bathroom."

-- "& that's the last thing he said 2 U before U txted me?"

-- "Yeah."

-- "Ur sure?"

-- "Yes, I promise. I haven't heard a thing from him since & I'm seriously about to start freaking out here!"

-- "Alright, calm down."

-- "I'm gonna go over 2 his house & see what's going on, okay?"

-- "Ok..."

-- "Just sit tight. I'll let U know when I find out what's going on."

I never actually got the chance to get back with her. By the time I arrived at his house that day, Rhonda was the last thing on my mind.

I got there right as about three EMSs and two police squads showed up. I'd seen and heard them tailing me as

I was rounding the curve to his house. I remember how bad my heart jackhammered against my chest. In three seconds flat, I silently prayed to every God I could think of to PLEASE let Craig be okay. God or whoever apparently wasn't taking requests because the sight that greeted me as soon as I opened the door to his apartment made me spill my own guts all over the floor until I felt about as empty as he, or what was left of him, looked.

Splayed across the floor of the living room was Craig's body, hollowed out, stretched, and deflated. His body looked like a goddamn exploded water balloon, with a gigantic red hole in his stomach. From this hole was this wide, sort of trail of his blood, coming out of his stomach and leading right out through the back door. It took them about an hour to hose him off the walls and everything.

Since that day, the story's been released all over the news. Obviously, nothing about the weight loss experiment he took part in was mentioned, and like I said, they CLAIM they're still searching for the cause of what happened. The thing is, I'm almost willing to bet they know as well as I or anyone reading this does that it had something to do with whatever that "microorganism" thing is they stuck in him. I can't prove it outright—not yet—but I'll say this much: there aren't any other reliable explanations.

The last thing I have on all of this is the 911 recording they showed on the news broadcast. Given the strange nature of the case as a whole, they felt it needed to be shown publicly. Usually, I'd have been against something like this, but in this instance, I can't help but be a little bit grateful for them doing this.

<u>Wednesday</u>

<u>(recorded 911 call -- time unspecified)</u>

-- "911, what is your emergency?"

-- (Voice is low, groaning) "I... I think I need an ambulance."

-- "Alright sir, can I get your name and address?"

-- "C-Craig... Craig Donovan..." (sounds of hurling are heard in background) "Oh-Oh God..."

-- "Craig, sir, are you still there?"

-- "I just threw up blood..."

-- "Okay, sir, we need your address."

-- "One... 1136 Whitmore... Lane..." (Thump is heard in the background, followed by agonizing shrieks) "Fuck! Oh God, it hurts!"

"Sir? Craig, can you hear me? What's going o--"

-- "It's... Fuck, something's trying to burst out of my stomach!"

-- "Alright, just stay on the line for me, okay? We're tracing the call to your location now. A unit will be dispatched and--" (Operator is interrupted by another shriek of pain on the other end) "Sir? Sir, can you still hear me?"

-- "OH GOD, WHAT THE FUCK IS THIS?! IT'S RIPPING OUT OF MY--" (Loud thump is heard, followed by sounds of wet squelching)

-- "Sir? Sir are you still there? Say something if you can hear me. Craig?"

(Line goes dead)

"Mother, May I?"

Warmth passed over Mark's chest with the baby-soft skin of her palm, causing him to shiver. A light moan escaped his lips.

She chuckled, leaning in close to his ear. "You're so eager, aren't you?"

"Y-Yes, Mother," he replied with a shaking breath.

Her nails began to dig into his flesh, and another moan, louder, erupted from him. This elicited a giggle from his mistress.

Her hips slid so smoothly against his, the bottoms of her thighs massaging his hips. "Tell me what you want, dear," she whispered, pushing her nails further into his chest. His heart tried to push itself against her palm with every palpitation. Her nails were dangerously close now to piercing his flesh.

She wouldn't allow that, though.

Not yet.

Mark's chest heaved and fell in rapid quakes, almost hyperventilating. She took him by his ear lobe, delivering a sharp, firm, yet playful bite while cooing to him. His breath seized altogether for about five seconds before his hyperventilation returned.

"What do we say, Mark?"

He didn't reply. Her nails started to pull away from their chosen divots in his chest. "P-Please..." he cried through his breaths.

"Aw," she teased, "Please what, baby boy?"

"Please... Please bleed me, Mother."

Her nails dug back into his skin. His gasps burst in large, desperate gulps. Further and further, her nails pushed until, finally, a small crimson stream flowed from his left breast. The thumping of his heart wore at his ribcage as it continued quaking, climaxing blood from the punctures.

She smiled, dabbing one of the streams with her index finger and bringing it to her tongue. "Mmm... You know how much I love your taste, baby boy."

His eyes met hers, yet he couldn't see her through his blindfold. Nonetheless, he could mentally picture the exultant grin she must've worn when she spoke. This was her favorite thing to do with him—which made it his by extension.

His chest pushed outward, presenting itself for her to access even more easily. It was a needless gesture but an appreciated one—her obedient little boy.

His hands started to move up her body from her thighs. She promptly stopped them before they could reach her hips. Her hips likewise ceased moving. "What do we say if we want something, Mark?" she asked sternly.

"M-Mother... Mother, may I?"

Chuckling, she slowly released her hold of his hands. "You may, baby boy."

His hands snaked up her hips, savoring the feeling of the tight satin dress she wore, something she did *just* for him, trying to feel her skin through it. While he explored, she leaned in close to his chest and fixed her mouth to his punctures. Her tongue was a snake, burrowing into every opening her nails had created. Her teeth acted as a steel vice, forcing the blood to ooze from the punctures.

Their moans synchronized, hers being muffled around his skin while his was projected throughout the room. Mark's heart punched against her nose as though it were trying to force her off of him—as if her penetration of his breast was a molestation—a rape of his very heart.

Whether his heart wanted it or not, though, *he* would not remove her. His hands grasped her buttocks, reigning her closer to him.

She rose, her lips lined with crimson. Moaning, she asked him, "You want to look at me?" Her palms rubbed gently across his chest. "You want to see how much you please me?"

"Y-Yes please. I-I want to look at you. I want to see you!"

"Then all you need to do is ask," she replied, her grin stretching even wider.

"Mother, may I please see you?"

Giggling, she replied, "Of course, baby boy." She then removed his blindfold.

His sight was slow to recompose, but his eyes grew to twice their size when it did. On his lap was Mother, the beautiful balm he'd idolized from birth, but now with her lips torn from one ear to the next, parted upward in a Glasgow grin. Her eyes pierced into his while her tongue wormed around outside of her mouth, eager like his twitching hips were now.

Her hands moved across his chest, then passed to his nipples, gently encircling them with her index finger. This made his chest thrust upwards. Her voice, no longer warm and seductive, more eager and animalistic to match her new bestial appearance, goaded him, "Go on, baby boy, I know you want to touch, don't you."

"Yes, Mother. I want to, no, I need to feel you!"

Her palms moved slowly from his chest to his throat. There, she began to squeeze.

"Mmm... Yes... Yes, I can feel it."

Her hips resumed their earlier motion with increased speed and intensity. Her hands guided his from her hips up to her torso.

Mark's hands moved to the top of her dress on their own. For just a moment, he allowed his hands to brush ever so slightly over her exposed cleavage, allowing himself a small taste of the ecstasy lying under the dress. Seeing this, Mother laughed. Her baby boy's innocence was always so adorable. The same was true for all her children, all her baby boys, born from her, and taken back into her. They'd all satisfied her hunger, and now Mark, the youngest of her children, would be the last. She would be whole again with him, and he would belong to her completely again.

"Mother, may I..." His gasping breaths, brought on by Mother's constant caresses, hindered him from finishing at first. She giggled again.

"May you what, baby boy?"

"Mother, may I touch you?"

"You may," she replied with a demonic cackle. Her eyes when she said this changed into those of serpents, slitted and jaundiced. He could feel a distinct heat bear down on him when he looked into them. "Oh, my sweet baby boy... All grown up now, and you've never been able to touch a woman like this, have you?"

"No, Mother," replied Mark. "The others bore me. They could never be as beautiful as you."

His words cause the torn ends of her mouth to split even further, ending just below her ear canals on either side. His hands begin to remove her dress. Before they were even exposed, his hands were kneading her breasts. She let out a soft moan that goaded him to knead even harder. Her hips now moved in a rapid cycling motion on his lap. She leaned down and lapped out her snakeish tongue. Its movement across his lips was almost ticklish to him.

Suddenly, her palm was pressed into his chest, and she whispered, "Give Mother a kiss, baby boy."

Without missing a beat, he leaned in, and their lips took hold of one another. They held for almost half a minute, her tongue tasting every inch of the inside of his mouth while he simply let her play before she broke away. He went back to kneading her breasts while she finished undressing.

Fully nude now, she pulled his head in between her breasts and asked, "Are you ready, Mark? Once this is done, you'll always be with me, and we'll never be apart again. Our family will be complete."

Mark was silent, taking a moment to enjoy her flesh against his. He wasn't lying when he said no other was as beautiful as her. Sure, this wasn't his first occasion at intimacy, but only the first where his heart felt as though it belonged to whom his body was being given to. He could feel her nails slowly and softly drag down his back.

"Have I told you, baby boy, how it felt when I gave birth?"

He responded by tightening his embrace around her.

"It was painful. I had to tear myself apart to give you all life. Because I'm not like the rest, I can't give birth the way the others do. I can't love a man and produce his offspring, you see? But I wanted someone I could hold. Someone I could love and lust with. That's why I gave life to you and your brothers by tearing my own flesh apart."

She pushed him back in his chair again and pointed to her left side, revealing three long scars that reached from around her back. Two of them were faded almost completely, but the last was still fresh, a deep red slash across her otherwise perfect body.

"Your brothers have joined back with me. Now it's your turn if it's what you truly want, baby boy."

"Yes please, Mother. I want to be with you again!" Her hands fell to his chest and again massaged just above his heart.

"Say it, then."

Mark took a deep breath and asked, "Mother, may I join you again?"

Without another word, Mother's jaws unhinged before sinking into his skull. A sharp cry of pain echoed throughout the room, but Mark did everything he could not to struggle. This was it, everything he ever wanted. To be one with the one who loved him—truly loved him. His scalp was ripped from his head, taking chunks of his brain with it, then spat out. Mark instantly became dizzy. Mother was now little more than an albino blur amidst a sparsely lit void.

A red filter quickly overtook what little he could see. Dark curtains formed at the outer edges of his eyes and slowly crept closer and closer to the centers. Mother focused now on the rest of his body: his chest, shoulders, and waist. All of it was quickly flayed open with her nails and teeth, exposing all of his inner organs, which she gleefully devoured. No part of them was left untouched. Even his bones were broken and gnawed upon until tender enough to swallow.

By this point, Mark had lost consciousness, his eyes hanging half-open and his lips frozen in a half-hearted smile. Mother had just managed to break open his rib cage when she found his heart still faintly beating. Wasting no time, lest she run the risk of it failing before she had the chance, she lunged forward and ripped it out of his chest with her jaws. It gave a further five hundred beats while she crushed and ground it with her teeth before finally swallowing it. Once this was finished, she rose again and took a deep breath.

What remained of her baby boy was not more than a tattered carcass. For just a moment, Mother's eyes burned. Her baby boy, the one she'd nurtured for over eighteen years, was no longer there, no longer able to nuzzle and nurse with his dearest Mother. But now, she knew, he was always with her, always a part of her again. She looked to her side and smiled at the sight of the last scar now faded.

After all, it was what he wanted, what he asked for, and his Mother always provided for her baby boy.

BEASTS IN THE SHEETS

Music blasted in the background, drowned out by Lillian's moaning. She thrust and thrust on him, slamming her hips down onto his, landing with such a brute force that made it somewhat painful for Trevor—not that it made a damn bit of difference to him. What was the fun if there was no challenge, right?

Lillian's moans grew, as did the ferocity of her movements. Trevor grunted, thrusting his hips upward. Passion, aggression, bloodlust—all of these surged throughout his body the more his body thrust. He felt like more than a simple animal. He was a *machine*, thrusting and thrusting, seemingly unable to stop. Her moans for him spurred him, drove him. He wouldn't stop until she cried his name, begging for mercy with tears in her eyes.

Lillian wasn't cracking, though. She simply continued making eye contact with him. She wasn't so easily impressed by the likes of Trevor. He was a young little punk, a little boy, thinking he had enough to swing around. She continued to pound harder and harder. Trevor began to wince. She smirked.

I tried to warn you, little boy, she thought to herself while yet another moan escaped her lips. Trevor began gasping. Soft groans of pain escaped from him as if she were pressing his chest as well as his pelvis. His eyes met hers. He could see the smug look of dominance on her face.

He would've taken this as "challenge accepted," except that no sooner than the thought of unleashing every bit of pent-up rage, frustration, and overall angst out on this little Barbie doll who was riding him, a strange pain erupted from his crotch.

It was so sudden, abrupt, and overwhelming that his body began to seize at once. Another, louder groan of aching pain shot from his mouth. This made both Lillian's smile and her moans grow. She was in paradise, while poor Trevor's sudden aching began subjecting his body to various states of Hell. So intense was the pressure, the feeling of jagged glass shards dragging across his genitals, that his vision began distorting. Lillian's face soon started to change, twisting and morphing from sensational, or "Fuckin' hot," as he always so bluntly put it, to something he wouldn't even recognize.

"Am I that good, baby?" he heard her chide him. He wasn't able to answer, forced only to stare at her, slack-jawed, while she stared maliciously back at him. She relished the look on his face, the priceless look of shock, confusion, amazement, terror, horror, and rue at his situation now. "Come on, cry for me, baby."

Her voice, while still smooth and seductive in a manner, began to take on a deeper pitch. Not a manly sort of baritone, but rather a simple trance-like one. It didn't sound like any woman Trevor had ever heard before. He was sure he'd never heard *anybody* that sounded like her before. It was frightening, actually, and yet so seductive in a strange sort of way. Somehow, he felt himself be lifted, in a way, out of his body. Think of the feeling of pulling off a sock or any piece of clothing. That would be the best description of what it felt like for Trevor to, quite literally, leave his own body and be *pulled* from it.

"What in the fuck?!" Was what he would've screamed had he any use of his tongue. As it was, Trevor found himself unable to feel his tongue at all. He could open his mouth, but no sound seemed to come. Then he realized it wasn't only his tongue he couldn't feel, but his body. His arms and his legs were completely numb to him. He may as well have not had arms or legs.

The only thing he managed to do was feebly open his mouth and see around him. The only parts of him he was aware of anymore were his inner thoughts, which were so riddled with panic, confusion, and just plain fear that he may well have wished that they had gone away before the feeling of his body. Around him, Trevor could see his bedroom. Everything looked how it was supposed to, except it all appeared red to him.

Everywhere he turned, every square inch of the room appeared washed in crimson light that looked as though it were glowing—like metal in a forge. Of course, his hearing seemed to stay with him as well, something he realized, to his dismay, when he heard a series of strange moans echo around and *through* him. His eyes were guided then back to his bed, where his jaw fell involuntarily in a way at the sight of his rigid, frozen body underneath a horrifying creature that just *barely* resembled a human woman at all.

Where he'd seen Lillian only moments before, there sat a furry, feral, animalistic-looking creature bearing long, sword-like protruding fangs and two horns curling to the back of her head. The only distinction that this thing was a female at all was the appearance of long, voluptuous breasts that bounced perfectly, gracefully in front of the petrified stare plastered all over Trevor's face. The moans soon devolved into echoing cackles, each blasting forth from her mouth each time she threw her head back in ecstasy.

When she did this, Trevor got his first glimpse of the face of this thing, this creature, this "true face" of his little old Lillian. Her face resembled a goat with slitted, jaundiced eyes. She bore the hooves of a goat. She'd told him there was a risk, that he wouldn't be able to handle it. But how in the hell was *he* supposed to know it would be *this* jacked up?

Unfortunately, ignorance wasn't going to spare him from his fate as he found himself drawn toward the creature on top of his body on the bed. He would've struggled like hell had he had any control over his consciousness. All too soon, though, Trevor found himself being sucked up like dirt by a vacuum cleaner into the creature's mouth. The only thing he could do was scream as the beast devoured his soul. Laughter, deep and distorted, quickly drowned this out.

The music raged outside, blasting up and down the street corner. At either side of the house, two ten by twenty foot surround sound speakers proudly shook the ground with each bass blast that the music emitted. At least sixty to seventy unruly punks shook their asses while teasing anyone who wanted to try getting handsy with them.

One of them, Craig Wilhelm, looked up at the top floor window on the right, seeing that the strange red light was still on. He frowned. *Huh... You know, I don't remember him having a red light like that.*

"Craig!"

His attention was ripped away from the window when he saw his girlfriend, Clarissa, looking at him, alarmed.

Instantly, before she could say anything, a cloud of smoke from the grill he was supposed to be manning billowed up his nostrils, gagging and making him hack his lungs up.

"Craig, what the fuck're you doing? You trying to burn us all alive?"

Once he finally stopped wheezing and began to breathe properly again, Craig replied, "Sorry, I, uh... Shit, I got distracted." He put on an awkward "Oopsie-daisy" while rubbing the back of his neck.

Clarissa gave him a look that said, "Really, dude?" before stomping to the grill, pushing Craig to the side. "Move!" she groaned annoyedly. "I'll grill the hot dogs and shit. You just... I don't know, go smoke or something. I'll be the useful one."

Craig's somewhat humorous, awkward face fell into a look of hurt. Clarissa saw this, sighed, and walked over to Craig, saying with a renewed smile, "But you're *my* idiot." She winked and landed a prolonged, wet peck on his left cheek, which renewed a bit of the joy lost in the mishap from a second ago. "Now go on, have fun."

"Okay," he replied, grinning. He winked, blew a kiss, and nodded toward the back of the yard as he joined the rest of the chaos and shouted, "Hey, I'll be waiting." As he stepped back, he looked up again at the window. The thought crossed his mind again to check on his buddy, only to be quickly overshadowed by falling backward into the backyard swimming pool. As he pulled himself out, though, he swore he heard the sound of screaming coming from somewhere in the house.

As out of their minds as everyone was, it shouldn't have been a complete surprise that no one else noticed (or at least seemed to mind) the noise. It was a party, and partygoers screamed when they wanted to, right? God knew the neighbors would say that it'd been going on all night, hearing at least a hundred people howling, all at the same time. This should've been normal for Craig, yet something about it seemed off to him.

While focusing on the window, Craig watched the crimson glow dissipate until it went dark. Craig frowned at this.

Maybe I should text him and make sure he's alright up there. Of course, the problem with that idea was that his phone was in his pocket and got submerged in the pool. *Fuck!* He thought before getting the idea to ask one of the many others at the party for one of their phones. Most either told him to fuck off or simply ignored him, but one girl made herself an exception.

"Hey, uh, listen, I was a dumbass and fell in the pool, ruining my phone. You mind if I borrow yours for a sec—" He cut off mid-sentence, transfixed by the beauty of the young girl before him. Her aqua-teal baby blues made Craig's heart jackhammer in his chest. Her long, luscious dark hair flowed in the wind, giving her the familiar "babe in the woods." Her D cups and thin waist compressed in just the right ways by a bikini that was likely a size too small sent a raging fire alight in between the young punk's legs.

She smirked mischievously.

"Well, hey there, baby girl," he started.

She said nothing as she brushed her hair behind her ear innocently.

Craig strutted over to her, puffing out his overworked pecs like he was showing off for a powerlifting competition. "What're you doin' all by yourself?"

Her smile widened. "Oh, nothing," she replied in an obviously fake tone.

"Nothin' huh?" Craig asked smugly.

She shrugged, snickering, never taking her gaze from his eyes.

Craig continued closer, almost unaware he wasn't even telling his body to move. "Well, uh... You wanna do somethin'?"

"Well... What'd you have in mind, big guy?" She winked after saying this, biting her lips to sell it.

Craig couldn't resist this. He *never* could resist a smokin' babe *throwing* herself at him like this *(Hell, what punk like him COULD? A little T&A never hurt anybody, right—regardless of a girlfriend?).* "I mean, you wanna have some fun, honey? We can take this up there..." He pointed to the upper floor of the house.

She giggled and replied, "You're on. I wanna warn you, though, things get pretty messy with me." She winked again after saying this. A classic trap—akin to telling a man, *"Don't be ashamed to admit you're a dead lay, hee-hee."* As mentioned before, this was next to impossible for any guy his age to resist, and unfortunately, Craig was no exception.

Puffing out his chest even further, Craig said, "Honeybun, if I had a dollar every time a chick's told me that before I had 'em screaming my name, I'd be rich enough to be throwing parties like this at *my* place."

"Oh, is that right?" she asked, raising her eyebrows. "Well, let's see if you can make *me* scream for you."

Craig's mouth stretched into an eager, wolfish grin. *Oh yeah, baby...* he thought, eyeing her up and down, imagining his head buried between those luscious tits of hers while her playboy-modeled ass bounced up and down on the hard-on that'd spontaneously grown in next to no time flat. *I'll make you scream, alright...*

"What's your name?" she asked, biting her lip.

"Huh?" asked Craig.

"Your name, tell me what it is so I know what to scream."

"Oh, uh, Craig."

She got up and walked up to him, meeting him at chest level, before shooting out her hand to snatch his crotch, squeezing it. Craig let out a slight yelp of pain.

"Well, Craig," she said, making her voice deeper and more voluptuous. "Why don't we go upstairs so you can show me what you're packin' in there?" She sold this by landing a peck on his cheek and a playful lick to his face.

Removing her hand from his crotch, she gingerly took his hand and guided him up to the house. At this point, Craig was so deeply enthralled by this beautiful little bombshell that he didn't realize Clarissa was watching him.

The fuck is he doing?! She watched as this little *Vampira* wannabe-looking bimbo led *her man* inside the house by his hand. *Who the hell is SHE?!*

"Hey!" she shouted. "The hell do you think you're going?!"

Craig paid no attention, his mind utterly oblivious to the world around him. The tramp guiding him gave a wink and raised her eyebrows before disappearing with him into the house. *Oh, hell no!*

Dropping the tongs right there, she immediately started after the two. However, just before she could reach the door, the girl slammed them shut in her face, quickly throwing the latch to lock them shut. Briefly, Clarissa saw the tramp stick her tongue out while flipping her the bird. Clarissa feebly tried jerking the sliding door open, but it made no difference.

The girl and Craig disappeared further into the house, heading upstairs. Just two seconds from seeing red, Clarissa stormed around to the front of the house.

In the room upstairs, just down the hall from the master bedroom, Craig was made by the girl to lay on the bed while she slowly stripped down in front of him, teasing him. Craig felt jolts of electricity fire off in his hips, causing them to shoot upward, eager to thrust inside the girl. She saw this, and her grin doubled, almost stretching across her face. She had him. He was hers, and he didn't even realize it.

(Nothing like a brainless little boy toy to make things fun, right?)

When she was fully nude, she slowly approached the bed, climbing onto and straddling Craig, making sure not to take his clothes off just yet. No, he would have to earn that pleasure. After all, wasn't he supposed to make *her* scream?

"You want it, baby?" she asked in a voice that droned a bit in Craig's ears.

Fuzzy and addled as his brain may have been, Craig noticed this the same way he'd noticed the red glow and the screaming coming from the master bedroom before—odd, out of place...

Wrong...

Still, his body remained limp, his brain caught in a noose tied by his balls. He nodded like an excited puppy in response to her question, saying, "Mhm-hmm!"

She leaned down close to his ear and whispered, "You sure? There's no shame in backing down now..." Her tone of voice contradicted this rhetoric. His eyes told her he wouldn't back down, causing her to snicker. She loved it when they chose to challenge her. There was nothing like putting another little boy in their place.

She licked his earlobe before clamping it between her teeth and tugging playfully. A soft moan escaped his lips. She whispered, "I hope you're ready. The beast is coming, and it's hungry." She snickered and moaned in his ear, "*So fucking hungry...*"

She pulled away from his ear, raising up and fully mounting herself upon him, keeping him fixed stiff with a fiery, primal stare. She started by caressing his chest through his shirt before undoing the buttons to expose his chest. "Ooh…" she crooned, "So strong, aren't ya?" She giggled playfully. "But do you think you're strong enough?" The more he listened to her voice, the more Craig began to recognize something strange about it, namely how it continued getting deeper and deeper, distorting more and more until it barely sounded human.

She lowered down to his chest, unhinging her jaws, exposing, for the first time, two sets of dagger-like canines. Craig had only enough time to make his eyes go wide with panic before she sank her teeth into his chest. Craig could only gasp, his lungs so shocked that anything more was physically impossible. Every muscle in his body convulsed at once.

The girl remained unphased by his body's reactions to her. *That's right, buck me all you want. You wanted this, and you're mine now anyway…*

She took her time, worrying her long, slender, incredibly moist tongue around the holes her teeth had punctured, savoring the warm, salty, metallic liquid. Eventually, she rose again, a vulpine grin on her blood-smeared lips. When Craig looked up, the smoking hot babe he thought he was about to score with was replaced with something that didn't even look like a chick at all, aside from her engorged, naked breasts and long, flowing dark hair.

In place of the rest were features similar to a goat, with two large horns curling out from her forehead. Her legs were now those of a goat as well. Craig opened his mouth to scream, "What the fuck," but found himself unable to say anything other than, "What are you?!"

To this, she laughed; this time, the laugh was completely devoid of humanity, sounding more like the laugh of a deep-voiced hyena, if such could ever exist. "You can call me Morrigan. I want you to scream it when I strip you of your soul. Think you can do that for me, baby boy?"

Her low and mesmerizing voice conveyed a tone of dominance to him, making him look upon her in even greater fear. He was screwed now, doomed to suffer at the hands of... of *whatever* the hell this-- this *thing* was.

The room around him started to glow red, similar to what he'd seen earlier in Trevor's room. The air began to slowly get heavier and heavier, causing him to gasp desperately.

"Mmm... Savor every breath, baby, you're gonna need it, he he." She ripped open the front of his jeans and lowered herself down onto him, ignoring his pitiful attempts at resistance. She went slow at first before gradually gaining speed and force in her movements. Before even a minute was over, Craig felt an excruciating stinging sensation shooting from his crotch. He cried out in pain, only to be drowned out in Morrigan's manic laughter.

"Craig!" shouted Clarissa. "Craig, you'd better get your ass down here *right now* and explain yourself!" There was no response from the upstairs hallway. *That asshole's really gonna make me come up there to drag him out.*

She began stomping up the stairs, her head pounding, seething with rage. By the seventh or eighth step, her anger gradually gave way to confusion when she heard groans of pain and strange laughter instead of cutesy giggling or moans of passion. *What the hell are they even doing up here?*

Then, a foul odor quickly captured her attention once she'd reached the top step. She knew the stench instantly when she caught it, but she didn't want to admit it. It was the stench of decay, of rot, of a long, desiccated corpse. Her heartbeat picked up speed and intensity.

"Cr-Craig?" she called out softly, her voice shaking now. One small step at a time, Clarissa made her way into the darkened hallway, lit only by an ominous scarlet glow coming from the room across from the master bedroom. From there, she also heard another shriek of pain getting drowned out by maniacal laughter.

"Craig!" She broke into a slight sprint and made it halfway down the hall before being stopped in her tracks. In front of her, coming out of the master bedroom, was what looked to be a giant, two-legged goat monster who was dragging a body behind her. Paralyzed with shock, Clarissa made no motion to run or hide. Her body remained rooted, frozen where she stood, hoping only that, by standing perfectly still, she wouldn't be noticed.

Sure enough, her hopes were granted, and the creature continued toward the adjacent bedroom. Squinting her eyes, she could make out just faintly through the red glow from the other room, the face of Trevor, forever preserved in a state of sheer terror, on the body being dragged across the floor. It was amazing that she could even tell it was him, given how shriveled and pasty his skin looked all over. He looked like a corpse after at least three or four months of decomposition. But how could that be possible?

This was but one of the million other questions swirling furiously around Clarissa's mind, the most pressing of which included, but weren't limited to: What the fuck was this thing that just came out of this room? Why's the room glowing? What happened to Trevor? Oh, and lest we forget, what's going on with Craig?

Despite that last one wanting to urge her forward, she remained frozen. The creature grabbed the doorknob and threw open the door, allowing a flood of scarlet luminescence to paint the hallway. This was swiftly followed by distorted moans of pleasure mixed with ever-fading groans of agony. "Room for one more?" she heard a voice, low and mesmerizing in pitch, ask with a demented giggle.

"Of course, dear sister," replied another similar, though not as low-toned, voice. "Better hurry, though, I think this one's fading fast."

What the? There's another one? She thought, panic starting to force her muscles back into action again. *What're they talking about, "He's fading fast"? Who's he?* Then, it struck her. She remembered how she'd seen Trevor being led inside the house in a similar fashion as Craig and then saw his pasty, shriveled carcass discarded on the hallway floor. Clarissa realized that her boyfriend, "*her* idiot," was about to have the same thing happen to him unless she did something quick. But what exactly?

Looking back to the stairs behind her, she thought of making a break for the kitchen and grabbing the sharpest knife she could when her eyes caught sight of something else closer to her. Just to her right, outside the hallway closet, sat a metal *Louisville Slugger* propped against a vacuum cleaner. The knife, she knew, would be deadlier. But time was of the essence, and judging by the way she could hear Craig's cries becoming weaker, she knew he couldn't wait that long.

With the speed of a leopard, Clarissa seized the bat and charged toward the room. She stopped, however, on the threshold, immediately paralyzed at the sight before her. On the bed, the disgusting goat creature that'd passed her in the hallway, as well as another slightly taller one, was mounted atop her boyfriend, one slamming down on his hips while the other rested over his face, smothering him. Craig's arms and legs could be seen weakly flailing for dear life, but it was of no impedance to the goat women.

"Let him go," Clarissa demanded, at first in a normal tone. When she saw that they weren't paying her attention, she raised the bat and screamed. "I said get off of him!"

One of them, the one from the hallway, turned around to see Clarissa. The goat creature looked shocked, the way anyone would look if caught in this situation, regardless of her demonic appearance.

Clarissa's back stiffened, her fingers tightening around the bat's handle.

The other one also looked up, carrying her partner's same look of surprise. "What in Satan's name is this?" asked the one from the hallway. "I thought you said we were alone in the house, Morrigan!"

Morrigan hissed at Clarissa, dismounting from Craig's face. "Lillith, you finish lover-boy here. I'll take care of her." Morrigan bounded from the bedpost toward Clarissa, spearheading her and tackling her to the floor. Restraining her target to the floor by her wrists, Morrigan seized Clarissa by her throat, instantly starting to crush it. Clarissa could hear her vicious growls as her goatlike face quickly became blurred. "If you wanted to play, too, you should've asked and waited your fucking turn, bitch," Morrigan growled. "But that's okay. I like playing with other girls, too." She then devolved into a hysterical cackling fit as the light slipped further and further from Clarissa's eyes.

Much of her vision was gone, reduced mainly to a broad cloud of red in her eyes. Despite this, though, she could still, out of the corner of her eye, see the body of her boyfriend going limp.

N-No... Craig!

The red glow from the room started burning brighter and brighter. The heat became more and more intense.

Using what strength she could summon, Clarissa firmly planted her thumbs into the goat creature's eye sockets.

Morrigan reeled away from her, howling in pain. Without wasting an instant, Clarissa took up the bat again and immediately went full throttle on Morrigan. Her strikes were ruthless, each one accompanied by a battle cry and making a distinct crack every time they connected with Morrigan's skull.

She didn't stop until she saw that the creature wasn't moving, a pool of blood pouring around her deformed head. Her attention then fixed on the other one, Lilith, who seemed too focused on her debauchery to notice that her sister was now a bloody, broken heap on the floor. Clarissa used this to her advantage, quickly and quietly ambushing the creature from behind and bracing the bat against her throat, strangling her.

Lilith was immediately thrown into a frenzy, bucking and thrashing like a bull rather than a goat. Her flailing was no match for Clarissa. She was pressed against the wall, holding Lillith trapped against her body, unable to buck or thrash around any further. Lilith attempted to gasp for any sort of breath, but with how tightly Clarissa had the bat braced against her throat, it was only a matter of time before her body, too, began to go limp. Clarissa took the opportunity to quickly wrap her hands around Lillith's face and snap her neck.

Lilith fell limp to the floor. For a moment, Clarissa stood breathless over the bodies of the two goat monsters. She'd done it. She'd killed them.

Craig!

She looked over to the bed. There lay Craig, nude, dazed, and groaning. "Craig!" she cried out, rushing to the side of the bed and shaking him. "Craig, come on, baby, wake up!"

"Cl-Cl-Clarissa?" he muttered softly.

"I'm here, it's okay." She started pulling him up from the bed, sending shockwaves of pain throughout his body.

"I can't," Craig whined. "It hurts to move my legs. Oh God, my legs."

"Okay, hold on, I'm gonna call the ambulance." She frantically dug through her pocket before pulling out her phone and panic dialing 911. The dial tone rang for about thirty seconds, each one sending her further into the clutches of a heart attack. *Come on, come on, PLEASE pick up!* Finally, the line connected.

"911 operator, what is the nature of your emergency?"

"Hello, I-I need an ambulance right now! My boyfriend can't move, and we've just been atta—" She felt a rough hand grab ahold of her mouth from behind, silencing her.

"You know…" said a deep, echo-y voice that, while familiar to her as Craig's, sounded low and droning, mesmerizing, just like Morrigan's and Lillith's. The hand wrapped around her mouth was also similar to those of the goat women. "It wasn't nice to interrupt bonding time with my sisters like that."

Panic immediately set in, but Clarissa quickly found any resistance was useless, this one having the grip of a gorilla on steroids.

Using one eye to peek behind her, she found the horrific sight of Craig. But added to his stud-muffin face, with its green eyes and granite-chiseled jawline, he also wore the face of a goat with large tusks protruding from his bottom jaw. A tear rolled down her cheek, which he sinisterly licked away with a devious grin.

"Like my sister said, bitch, if you wanted a turn with me, you should've asked." Those were the last words she would ever hear. The only sounds piercing her ear drums after that were the cacophonous mixes of deranged cackling and agonized wailing.

The music raged on outside as every partygoing punk lost themselves to booze or weed, if not both. Occasionally, one or two would look up at the top floor window, see the auroral red glow emanating from it, and smile. *Somebody's gettin' it on*, they'd think before losing themselves again. A few would even overhear the cackling and moaning from up there and would whistle and catcall like a bunch of lunatics. Perhaps they felt jealous, perhaps not. One thing was for certain, though: whoever they were, they must be really *freaky in the sheets, huh?*

CLEANING THE BASEMENT

That basement was the nastiest one I'd seen by far. Dust bunnies, cobwebs, and I'm pretty sure black mold covered each corner, running up the creases and halfway up to the ceiling. *Seriously, how the hell do these people live like this?*

I'd be lying if I said I hadn't at least considered calling the housing department and letting them have a look at this shit. Then again, I guess that's what *I* was for. To keep them from having to get off their asses for it.

Anyway, I went in and was immediately hit with the foulest smell possible. We're talking about the combined smell of cow shit, rotted meat, sewer water from the Hudson, and a decaying body, all mixed in a blender. Let that colorful image sink in for a moment, and then be thankful you didn't have to smell it. I took up the pressure washer I had with me, cranked it all the way up, and went full throttle on the entire place.

I'll tell you, the way that shit didn't want to come off the walls...

And you know, it wasn't just dirt or mildew, either. There were also a whole bunch of these weird stains, some of which I was afraid were blood or maybe shit. I was hoping for the latter if I were made to choose between the two. God knows I didn't need to be stumbling into a damn murder scene.

Something else that made the job that much more annoying was the fact that the place was so huge. You'd think that with a basement that big, you might be able to keep it a little tidier, right?

Nope.

No, pretty much every square inch of the damn place was covered in fucking stains and mold. Even on the highest setting, I couldn't get it clear. A few spots here and there were about as good as I could get it after about 20 minutes of continuous blasting. Finally, I said screw that and went back to get my scraper. Thank God, too, that it was the extendable kind so I could use it from a distance instead of getting right up close and personal with any of that.

I got at it with the scraper and made a little more progress. Not much, of course, but at least enough to go back over it with the hose to clear it off completely. The stuff was thick, too, like I was scraping tar. It was dense and thick but strangely also rubbery and gelatinous. It sort of wiggled when poked with the end of the scraper, which just made my stomach gurgle all the more.

The constant squelching sounds I kept hearing every time I scraped didn't help, either. The smell eventually got to a point where I had to stop again to grab my dust mask, which only minimalized the stench by a small margin. Still, though, I wasn't a quitter, so I snatched my scraper back up and had at it again—albeit with a lot more vigor.

With this, I actually managed to clear away a good bit of the build-up along the wall in a little over an hour. With each jab, I noticed, whether out of just the sheer intensity of the shoveling or if the build-up wasn't as thick in certain areas, the stuff started coming off easier and easier. Seeing this only made the movements of my arms speed up more and more. I even let out an excited laugh; it was finally gonna be over with!

I made it all the way to the end of the wall, viciously hacking away the last bit of grime like a psycho. When I saw it leave the wall, I stepped back, threw my hands up, and exclaimed, "Finally, haha, it's finally over!" I was in the middle of the mad dash back toward the opening of the room to grab the pressure washer again when I stopped and noticed something.

The walls were covered again!

I damn near wanted to throw up again right then and there. What the fuck?! How did that shit get back on the walls?

I made the mistake of getting up close to the wall, enduring every bit of that horrid odor, to see whether or not I was just seeing things. Nope, that shit was right back where it was. It looked like I hadn't even touched the damn wall.

My body shook. I was sick, both mentally and quite physically, of this whole job. The adrenaline had already started to wear off, so my arm was also tired. I was not at all happy about this.

I turned around in a huff and started my way back to grab the scraper again. All the way there, I was grumbling about how I was going to, more or less, rip the fucking walls apart to get the stuff off this time. Along the way, though, I saw something happening with the stuff on the walls. About a foot or two away from my feet, I watched something small and black go zipping across the ground toward the wall. I looked at the wall but couldn't see anything, so I looked forward again and continued.

A couple more paces forward, and I saw it happen again, this time two of them. I managed to run up and spot one of the little blobs just before it could connect with the other on the wall. I then jabbed my scraper into it like a spear, holding it in place. I couldn't see much of anything of it, so I clicked on my shoulder flashlight to get a better look at it. When I did, my heart stopped, and this time, I did throw up a bit in my mouth.

The little sliver of gunk, or "stuff," was human tissue!

Pink and squirming, it looked like a big fat worm, but it wasn't. It was human skin, just scuttling along the ground like a mouse or a roach. Slowly, I turned the light to illuminate the wall beside me. The wall, large and spacious as it was, was covered all along its length with living, pulsating, writhing, disgusting human tissue. It undulated rapidly inward and outwards in accordance with the deep-pitched, yet still very much audible, heartbeat coming from it.

I couldn't believe it. ANY of it. It was there, though. It was real!

Actual human tissue, living and writhing around, all across the basement wall. Out of reflex, I spun around to see if the other wall was like this, and sure enough, it was. Then I looked up to see, to my horror, that it was above me as well. Directly overhead was a portion bulging downwards, looking like a plastic bag full of water ready to burst all over the top of my head. As it lowered further and further, I dove forward out of the way.

The more the bulge sank in front of me, the more it started to take another shape entirely. By this, I mean that the closer it came to the ground, the more I watched as two small lumps stretched themselves downward before morphing into what looked like a set of hands. Then, from the very top of the bulge, a smaller lump started poking outward, which then formed into a shape resembling someone's head.

That was where I drew the line and was ready to gun it the hell out of there. Fuckers could keep their money. I wanted no part of this job or this house anymore. I started to go full steam ahead when I was stopped dead by another bulge, this one coming out of the side of the wall. Like the one from the ceiling behind me, the one in front of me reached out with two long lumps that quickly shaped themselves into arms. I took two small steps back when my heart skipped about three beats from the deafening, unnatural screech that blasted from behind me.

I snapped around to look, seeing in front of me a full grown... I don't know, *a thing that looked like a person but without* skin. Imagine Mr. Goodbody, only it was real, just a grown man with no skin covering his beating, pulsing muscles. Its eyes were wide open, lidless, and *yellow!* Its jaw hung open like it had the jaws of an alligator, and it took all its strength to close its mouth.

The creature took a single, crooked, wobbly step forward, prompting me to take at least two or three steps backward. I stepped back until I bumped against something behind me—something wet and squishy. I didn't need to look back to realize I'd just backed myself into a trap.

The breath from the creature behind me was heavy, hot, and rancid, smelling exactly like the rest of the basement. I could hear its deep, guttural growling growing ever slowly in pitch. My own body shook violently.

My left eye wandered to the ground, just a few feet to my right, where the pressure washer was. My other eye remained frozen on the hideous thing standing in front of me, snarling and baring its needle-like teeth at me. My arms twitched.

The pressure washer was only a foot or two away. It wasn't much, but it was all I had. I could spray 'em like a couple of cats, drive 'em back at least long enough to make a beeline out of there and back to my truck. It was possible—unlikely, but possible.

Just a foot or two away...

Another lump started drooping from the ceiling just a couple of inches behind the one in front of me. I knew pretty soon they really would have me cut off. My other eye migrated with the other to the pressure washer. It was now or never.

Instantly, I dove to my right, landing headfirst and snatching up the pressure washer. The two creatures surrounding me dove after me, screeching like a couple of rabid dingoes with their naked, gangly arms outstretched to snatch at me. Without thinking, I managed to aim the end of the hose at them and blast them straight out of the air.

By then, the third one had already formed and was ready to join the party, so I took aim and let him have it, too. Before I knew it, about four or five lumps formed simultaneously from the ceiling, with about two or three more coming from the walls. The ones I'd waterlogged were already starting to stir, too, so I took my chance to leave by booking it full steam ahead toward the door. I didn't even bother bringing the pressure washer with me.

I'll say right now that those fifteen or twenty seconds, running like hell like that, were probably both the quickest and, at the same time, slowest seconds of my life. Time was almost nonexistent at that moment, almost like Limbo or purgatory or whatever they call it. Eventually, though, I found myself at the door, where I spear-threw myself out, landing face down on the grass, only to immediately bound back to my feet, slam the door, and latch it back before two of them could catch me.

For another thirty-something-odd seconds after that, I stood with my back braced against the door while they did their damnedest to bash it down. I can't say precisely how long that lasted, but I know it wasn't long before everything went quiet again on the other side of the door.

Even still, I kept myself against the door for a little longer, just in case.

At some point, of course, I finally moved away from the door and made yet another beeline for the truck, where I put the pedal to the metal faster than I ever had before or since back to the office building. I clocked out for the day just about as soon as I walked in, taking just enough time to go in, turn in my gear sans the pressure washer and scraper, and change back into my regular clothes. I only had about another half hour left of that day's shift anyways, plus the supervisor had already left for the day himself, so I didn't catch any shit for punching the clock early, either.

This was about three or four months ago, but I've had vivid nightmares ever since. We still get requests from that address to come out and "fix" the basement (notice I use that term loosely), which I don't respond to anymore. Trust me, there isn't, nor will there ever be, enough money printed ever to get me even to consider setting foot anywhere near that fucking place, MUCH less that basement.

JARED'S OTHER HALF

J ared stands in front of his mirror, which smiles back at him. He pulls on empty, loose-hanging flesh. He has one thought and one thought only as the thing in the mirror bellows with laughter at him: *When can this end?*

In his left hand, Jared holds the steak knife he grabbed from the kitchen. His hand shakes as he holds it. He doesn't want to do this, but is there any other choice here? He's already tried everything else, Lord knows. No, this is the only way. It tells him so itself. The thing in the mirror, the thing that *says* it's him—but goddamn it, *IT ISN'T!*

The blade is positioned across the middle of his bare chest. It won't take long, he thinks to himself. As gaunt as he's become, having already tried starving the demon out, he has no real cushion to protect his vital arteries. One way or another, It will end here and now. It has to. He presses the blade into his chest and begins to drag.

Several small crimson streams run down his chest in small, dark, thick rivulets. The pain is searing, but Jarod merely grits his teeth. He sees the creature in the mirror's vulpine grin stretch. He hears its voice boom in his ears.

"Yes Jarod, that's it... Let me out..."

Jarod closes his eyes. He fights back tears. He can't let the thing see him suffering. He can't let it see any weakness, not any more than it already has.

For a moment, just a moment, Jared stops. He wonders if he is making the right decision...

If I don't, I'll never be rid of him. But if I do...

He shakes his head and presses the blade against his chest again. This time, he's unable to keep a small groan from slipping from his lips. The creature's laughter echoes once more in his ear. *Just keep going!* He tells himself.

This HAS to end!

Jared had always loved making faces in the mirror from an early age. Like all kids, it amused him to talk to "the man in the mirror," make funny faces at him, talk to him about cartoons, and ask him what his favorite color was. Of course, one would see this and assume the poor kid's life was pretty damn lonely—and bully for them, that'd be one assumption they'd hit the nail hard on its head with. He'd never understood his peers, which in turn left him understood even less by them.

As bad as this was on its own, it was no better for him at home. Jared was an only child without a mother after her sudden and rather unexpected demise a month after he was born. His father wasn't ever around either, leastways not in any way that left the two any time to bond. This led to him meeting the "man in the mirror" for the first time.

He'd just turned five and was well accustomed to amusing himself by then. His favorite was sticking his tongue out in the mirror. It felt so satisfying for him. Why shouldn't it? He couldn't do it anywhere else without catching hell for it. Adults would've tanned his little behind while other kids on the playground or at school would've swung their foot in it if he did. The mirror, however, couldn't and wouldn't say or do anything. It would play along, making faces at him back. That was half of the fun of it.

The only catch was that, unlike his peers or adults, the mirror couldn't hold much conversation with him. He would say something to it, maybe ask it for advice on some simple predicament he'd found himself in (usually something having to do with how to get out of bath time or how to avoid getting cooties from the girls at school), but wait for an answer that ultimately wouldn't ever come. He'd sometimes make up a quote-unquote "voice" for a reply, but it wasn't the same, and he knew this.

Still, it seemed better to him than trying to talk to somebody else. At least he could say and do whatever he wanted with the mirror, even if it couldn't *actually* speak to him. That was until one day, when he was playing in the mirror, attempting to plaster his "scary monster" face to intimidate it, he heard it for the first time.

"Raar!" he shouted, curling his lips in to reveal his canines (his "Vampire teeth," as he always loved calling them)

"Hey, you look kinda funny."

Jared paused. *Huh?* He looked around the bathroom. *Who said that?*

"Dad?" he softly called out. There was no answer. He peered out into the hallway, finding it dark and empty. He looked back in the bathroom. Again, there was no one. He was alone.

"You like making faces, Bud?"

Jared's head snapped around the room once more. Now, he was *sure* he'd heard it that time. He noticed, too, that this wasn't his dad's voice. It wasn't even a grown-up's voice. It was small, like his own. Now that he thought of it, it sounded a lot more like...

"Do it again, Jarod. Make a face at me. I wanna see another."

He froze. Shivers broke out all across his body, causing the hair throughout to stand at constant attention. That wasn't just some kid's voice. No, it was HIS. It was like when he'd hear himself speak to his reflection in the mirror, except...

Except he *wasn't speaking!*

"Wh-Who's there?" he called out, shaking. For a moment, no one answered. He tried looking around again, but it resulted in the same thing as last time; he was alone in the bathroom, and no one else around him was speaking to him. No one, that is, except for himself.

"Oh, come on. You've seen me before, Jared. We play together every day, remember?"

"Where are you?" Jared asked.

"Where I've always been, ya goof."

He then slowly looked at the mirror. It was his reflection staring back at him—or at least, it looked like his reflection was staring back at him. Then again, last he checked, he was pretty sure that he didn't have a giant, rotund "Santa Claus belly" and was definitely sure that he had a face on his head. What stared back at him in the mirror, however, was the complete opposite.

Jared's eyes bugged. "What the?"

"Hello there, Jared," it said. Its voice was caught between a baritone, bestial sort of growl and a perverted mimicry of Jared's voice, making Jared's stomach turn over all the more. Jared heard the voice and could only imagine it elsewhere, coming from a person who was trying to talk to him while puking. "You remember me, don't you, Jared?"

Jared's head shook violently as he took two measured steps back.

"Wait, don't go." He stopped. "Please don't go. I just got here."

"O-Okay..." Jared replied, shaking. "W-Well um... uh, what-what do you want?"

"To play."

"Huh?"

"You know, just like you were a minute ago. Like you do every day."

"You mean making faces in the mirror?"

"Yeah, that, and talking to me and telling jokes like you always do."

Jared stood frozen for a moment. The air began to feel heavy in his throat as if it were forming a noose around his neck.

"Why do you look so scared? It's just me."

"Um... O-Okay but... I don't... Know you."

"What do you mean you 'don't know me?' I just told you who I am."

"Yeah but... But you can talk."

"Of course I can."

"But you didn't do that before."

"Sure I did. You just never really heard me until now."

Jared frowned. "What do you mean?"

"Well, think about it like this: you know how when you're a baby, you try to speak to your parents, but they can't understand you?"

Jared nodded cautiously.

"That's because that was me. See, I'm the deep down part of you."

"Deep down?" Jared asked. His eyes diverted then from the mirror to his stomach. A thunderous laugh roared from the mirror, driving Jared almost into jumping straight out of his skin. When he looked back at the mirror, the thing's blank head was thrown back while his belly bounced as a giant rubber ball would.

"Hey, what's so funny? And where's your face, anyway?"

The creature's laughter ceased abruptly, and Jared's back stiffened again.

"What'd you say?" it asked, agitation oozing from its voice.

"U-Um... Um, I-I just asked what was so funny..."

The creature growled, making Jared almost lose the minute control he somehow still possessed over his bladder. His knees quaked, threatening to buckle from beneath him and bring him crashing to the floor at any given second.

"Well, if you insist... I was laughing at how dumb you looked just now."

"What do you mean?"

The creature held up its hands in air quotes and mocked his voice, saying, *"What do you mean?"* What I *mean* is that you still can't understand me. Just now, you thought I was in your belly. No, Jared, I'm far deeper in you than that. I'm in your mind, your heart. I'm the other half of you—what you *really* are."

Jared backed away again. His eyes darted around the room. He needed a way out. This wasn't fun anymore, and he couldn't understand what the creature was telling him. *"The other half of me?"* What the heck is *THAT* supposed to mean?

"I uh... I uh..."

"I uh, uh, uh," the creature mocked. "You 'uh' what, huh? You wanna leave? Gee, no wonder you don't have any friends. As soon as someone starts to do *one thing* you don't like, just because someone looks a certain way, all of a sudden, you don't wanna play with 'em anymore. And here I thought you would've been taught a little bit better, eh?"

Jared's mouth hung slack, lost for words. What was there to say? He wasn't usually judgmental, sure. His paw had taught him a little better. But all the same, this was just… a little bit different.

Other kids weren't this weird, he thought to himself.

"Oh, and you wanted to see my face?" the creature asked, annoyance laced in its disgusting voice.

Jared's mouth moved, probably to tell him that he was good on that, that he *really* just wanted to go. But before any of that had a chance of being voiced, the creature pulled up his too tight for his stomach t-shirt, exposing two jet-black eyes staring back at him embedded in sockets of exposed sinew just below its flabby chest line. Jared's eyes doubled in size as his breath left him. A few inches below the thing's eyes, a seam split across the length of the mid-abdominal region and opened to reveal a cavernous maw, complete with what looked to Jared like over a hundred or more inlaid, needle-like teeth like those of a piranha, all embedded into meaty, sinewy gums.

"What the?" Jared cried breathlessly. The creature's mouth split further at the corners, extending its malicious grin. "What are you?" He found himself backed against the door.

"I've told you twice now, you little shit," growled the creature. By now, its voice had almost completely shed any resemblance to Jared's and sounded more like an ogre or a troll (that is, what he *imagined* either of these sounding like). There was just enough there, though, that still made Jared shiver. "I'm what should be on the outside, not you."

From where he stood against the door, Jared swore he could see the creature getting closer and closer to the edge of the mirror. Jared groped for the knob, constantly missing it due to being unable to look away from the mirror. Inch by inch, the creature approached the mirror, outstretching its hand. Its abysmal maw cracked open wider with each inch it came. Jared was trapped, nowhere to run or hide.

Finally, his hand managed to grasp the knob of the door, right as it looked like the creature's bulbous arm was about to penetrate the glass and snatch him up. In a single motion, Jared swung open the door and flung himself out, taking off and running back to his room. Once there, he slammed and locked his bedroom door before going under his bed to hide, a habit he'd taken up anytime he'd gotten scared ever since his father decided to teach him a lesson about staying in bed after lights out by chasing him back to his room.

(Lesson learned alright)

He huddled under the bed for almost twenty minutes before his senses kicked in, and he remembered that he was five, not two. He was too old to be hiding under the bed from the "big scary monsters"—especially ones from the mirror. Imagine if the other kids at school or on the playgrounds heard about this. He'd for sure have no friends—not until high school, at least.

He shook his head and pushed himself out from under the bed. *Stop bein' scared, you're a big boy, and besides, he was in the MIRROR, he couldn't hurt you.*

("But he came so close...")

Out from under the bed, he stood in the center of his bedroom and took a deep breath. *You're fine. There are no scary mirror monsters.*

("But... But he WAS there.")

There are no scary mirror monsters.

("He said he was INSIDE me.")

There are NO SCARY MONSTERS!

("But it was right there! It was coming for me! It was gonna—")

"Jared!" His head snapped around to see his father standing at his bedroom doorway. He looked spooked at his father.

"Oh uh... H-Hey dad," he stammered.

His father paused, frowning for a second. "Everything okay, sport?"

Jared hesitated for a second, darting his eyes around the room in a frenzy before answering that everything was fine.

"You sure?" his father asked, raising his eyebrow.

Jared nodded. "Uh-huh."

"Okay," his father said, not very convinced but unwilling to push the issue. It's probably just a kid thing; maybe he's just off in dreamland again or something, right? That's what he thought, anyway. "Well, if everything's okay, come downstairs and get your shoes on."

"Where're we going?"

"You don't remember? It's time to go see Mrs. Wendy."

"Oh yeah!" he exclaimed cheerfully. He rushed out of the room, past his father, and down the stairs.

His father smiled. He was probably the only kid in the world who enjoyed seeing a therapist this much.

It was true, too. He always loved seeing Mrs. Wendy, though it likely was less about getting psychiatric or behavioral therapy like his father was hoping for and more about getting to line his little pockets with as much candy as his little fists could fish out.

"So, how're things going at school?" Mrs. Wendy asked. " Are you having any better luck making new friends?"

Jared shrugged. "Eh, sorta, not really."

"Oh no?"

Jared shook his head.

"Why's that? Have you been using the strategies we talked about?"

"Yeah."

"Still nothin'?"

He shook his head.

"Hmm... Okay, well, have you been keeping yourself happy in spite of this?"

"Oh well... You know, the usual..."

Mrs. Wendy smiled warmly. "Still making funny faces in the mirror, huh?"

"Yeah..."

"What's the matter?"

Jared paused, attempting to shrink his head down into his shoulders like a turtle.

"Did someone make fun of you for it at school?"

"No..." He began to tuck his legs to his chest.

"Jared, you know you can talk to me, right?"

Jared nodded.

"What do we always say? If you're feeling scared or like you can't talk—"

"Then take a moment and breathe before you squawk," he finished.

"That's right. Now, deep breath in." They inhaled at the same time. "Now exhale, slow and steady." They both let out a cleansing breath. "Good, now tell me, what happened?"

"Well... It's just that, earlier, I was doing it, and well..." he trailed off, attempting to tuck his legs in again.

"What is it?" asked Mrs. Wendy.

"Well, it's just that usually, when I do it, the man in the mirror doesn't talk to me.

"Talk back to you?" she asked. "How do you mean?"

"You know, like actually talking to me." He saw from Mrs. Wendy's face that he wasn't making sense to her. "He started saying I looked funny when I made faces in the mirror at him."

"And what'd you say to him?"

"I... Well, nothing."

"Nothing?"

"Nuh-uh. I didn't want to."

"Why not? Was he mean?"

"Sort of."

"What'd he say that was mean?"

"He said I looked stupid and funny. He even called me a little... a little..." His head shrunk again.

"A little what, it's okay, you can tell me."

"He used a potty word."

"Oh, I see. Well, can you tell me what it means?"

"He said I was a piece of dog poop."

"I gotcha. Why do you think he said these things to you, Jared?"

Jared shrugged. "I dunno, but he tried to get me through the mirror, so I ran away."

"Hm... Okay..." She leaned back in her chair, narrowing her eyes. "What did he look like?"

"Well, he looked sorta like me, you know, except he was big and fat and blobby and his face was on his belly."

"On his belly?" Mrs. Wendy asked, her mind a mixture of confusion, concern, and a slight twinge of amusement. Children have the most humorous imaginations, don't they?

"Uh huh, and his mouth had lots of big sharp teeth, and he said he lived inside me."

"Hm... Inside you?" Jared nodded. "Did he say where?"

Jared pointed to his head and his chest. "He told me he lived in my head and my heart."

"Okay." After this, a moment of silence hung in the air, only broken by the clock ticking at the room's far end. Mrs. Wendy pulled out a stack of paper and crayons. "I want you to do me a favor real fast. Can you do that?"

"Uh... sure."

She pushed the paper and crayons in front of him.

"Think you can draw what he looks like for me?"

Jared glanced back and forth between Mrs. Wendy and the papers. "Um... Uh, okay." He took out the black crayon and began to draw. It didn't take him long—maybe about three to five minutes—before he set the crayons down and presented Mrs. Wendy with his illustration.

Mrs. Wendy frowned at first, leaning forward to get a closer look. "Well, he sure doesn't *look* friendly. I'll give you that."

"That's what I was saying. He was big and mean and scary."

"I'll bet."

"I don't want him to come back, but I don't know what to do."

"Hm. Is this the first time you've seen him?"

"Yeah, but he said something weird."

"Like what?"

"He told me he'd been in me since I was a baby."

"Really?"

"Uh-huh, and he said I only saw him now because I understood him." He sighed and dropped his head. "I don't know."

"Hey, it's okay. I'm going to help you, okay?"

Jared looked up at her. "You are?"

"Yep. Here's what I want you to do the next time you see him. I want you to look him straight in his face and say,

'You're mean, and I don't want you around.' Think you can do that?"

"I... I think."

"Here, try it with the picture."

Jared looked down at the drawing.

"Say it now."

"You're mean, and I don't want you around. Go away."

"Good, do it again."

"You're mean, and I don't want you around. Go away."

"Good, good. Now, say it proudly. Put some *oomph* into it. You want to make him go away, right?"

He nodded. "

Then you gotta make him understand that you don't want him around anymore. Try one more time, as tough as you can sound."

"You're mean, and I don't want you around! Go away, NOW!" Adrenaline started pumping in Jared's chest. He was doing it. He felt like he was conquering the beast right there and then. He felt like he would be ready for the next time he saw the monster, if ever.

He left happily with his father about a minute later and went home again. That night, little Jared was the happiest he could be. The rest of the night until supper was spent with him alternating between bogarting the TV and turning his little play area in the living room into a warzone with his G.I. Joe playsets. Eventually, though, nature's call reached him (no thanks to the six juice boxes he insisted on downing a few moments earlier), and he sprang up and bolted for the bathroom.

He made it just in time and was cleaning up when he heard the all too familiar, sickening laughter coming from the mirror again. This caught Jared off guard, but he wasn't about to jump again. He closed his eyes. *Just remember what Mrs. Wendy said.*

"Oh, Jared…" the creature cooed in a sing-song voice. We never got to play." Jared stiffened his back, drawing a deep breath in. Come on… Make faces. You look so funny when you do…"

"Listen," Jared said, opening his eyes and fixing the abominable creature in the mirror with a fierce, cold glare. "You're mean, and I don't want you around. Go away!"

A low, rumbling laugh bellowed from the mirror. "Aww, your feelings hurt, snowflake? Are you going to cry to mommy? Oh wait, that's right. You can't, can you?"

Jared didn't reply. He didn't flinch. He stood, still as stone, and continued staring daggers at the creature.

"Ooh, somebody's a *tough guy,* ain't they? Yeah, I better watch out, shouldn't I?" Laughter shook the floor around him, making his legs shake.

"I said I want you out, NOW!"

"And what if I don't feel like it, huh? What's your pudgy, bouncy little ass gonna do about it?"

Jared's body began to quiver, not in fright but in anger.

"You gettin' mad, tough guy, huh? You gonna do something or stand there looking at me with goo-goo eyes, faggot?"

That tore it. That wasn't just any curse word. No, that was one of *THE* curse words, and this ugly jerk just used it at him. Heck, he'd even made fun of his mom. Oh, if only he could take his fists and—

"I SAID GET OUT!" he screamed furiously while driving his fist into the mirror. The mirror cracked, and a few shards fell to the floor. For a second, just a second, Jared felt like the Incredible Hulk, surging with strength and power. He'd done it. He'd just conquered his bully. The creature was gone.

When he looked at his hand, all strength left him, and his jaw fell open. In his hand, embedded almost halfway with each, were multiple decent-sized shards of glass. Searing pain, almost on cue, shot throughout his arm, and he shrieked bloody murder. Blood was streaming out of punctures in his hand. Ten seconds later, Dad came rushing into the bathroom to see what was wrong, only to have his breath jump from his lungs less than a second after opening the door.

"Oh my God, Jared, what'd you do?!" he cried.

Jared, through tears, tried as hard as he could to articulate, but it was no good.

"Okay, stay here, I'm gonna get the ambulance." His father rushed downstairs, almost falling at the halfway point, and snatched the cordless telephone from its base. Three to five minutes later, the ambulance arrived, and Jared was rushed to the E.R., where he spent the next seven to eight hours enduring the excruciating process of getting stitches.

"Son, what were you thinking?" his father asked while the doctor applied bandages over the stitches.

"I... I had to..."

"What, what happened?"

Jared looked into his father's eyes. He could see the overwhelming panic brimming over in his eyes. He didn't want to lie, but then, would he believe the truth? Mrs. Wendy did, but that was different. She's *supposed* to believe him. Daddies are too, though, aren't they?

Jared's eyes grew anxious, and he said, in a small voice, "I had to make him go away."

"What?"

"I said I had to make him go away."

"Make who go away?"

"The man in the mirror." He grimaced the instant the words left him.

"Huh? What're you talking about, son?"

"There was someone in the mirror, and I wanted him to go away because he was being mean, so I did what Mrs. Wendy told me and—"

"Wait, Mrs. Wendy told you to do this? She told you to punch the mirror?"

Jared opened his mouth to speak, but it was of no use. By that point, his father had heard everything he needed to. "That's it, we're not going to be seeing Mrs. Wendy anymore."

"But wait, we can't. I like Mrs. Wendy. I don't want to stop."

"Enough, it's okay. We'll find another therapist for you. Hopefully, one who has the sense not to go telling little boys to hurt themselves."

Jared was about to cry out another objection but stopped when he caught his father's glare, his trademark "I have spoken, and the word is final, lest you'd like the belt across your hide" stare.

That was the last time he saw Mrs. Wendy, and for a long while after, the last time he saw his monstrous doppelganger, his so-called "Other half."

***

He stepped off the bus Friday afternoon, eager to get as far away from the bus, the obnoxious dipshits on the bus, and by extension, from the school altogether as possible. The week had been particularly rough, with back-to-back tests (ones he didn't bother studying for—because who does?) and gym class kicking the absolute dogshit out of him. Of course, there was the fact that he'd been grounded all week, thanks to the aforementioned shirking of his studies, earning him shitty grades on his report card for the quarter.

But now it was the weekend. Grounding was lifted just in time for his girlfriend's party that night. He rushed from the bus stop back to his house. There, he immediately stripped naked, tossing his clothes along the stairs haphazardly as he went along the stairs into the bathroom. The party started at 5:00, and it was just getting on 3:30. That was just enough time for him to shower, shave a bit (Rhonda wasn't too keen on the stubble while they had sexy time), find something cool to wear, hit the bowl a couple of times, and then hit the road.

He stumbled into the bathroom with his pants still around his ankles. In his craze, he paid no attention to the fact that the light was off and all kinds of clutter were littered across the floor, causing him to trip and bust his ass on the tiled flooring.

"Fuck!" he shouted. He picked himself back up, but when he did, upon seeing the mirror, he froze. He was looking into his mirror, the same as he'd always done in the mornings before school and evenings before bed for the past twelve and a half years, but what was looking back at him was definitely *not* him.

He was athletic-looking, having played on his school's football and track teams for the past three years. However, this thing in the mirror was anything but, with its bulging belly that looked like someone had stuck a giant wad of chewed-up chewing gum to the front of some guy's stomach. Odd as this was, weird as it was, it was far from what disturbed Jared the most. No, what disturbed Jared here was that the thing didn't have a face!

Well, leastways, not where a face *should've* been. Instead, the front of the thing's face was smooth and blank, while his stomach, on the other hand, the bulbous, gross potbelly of the thing, began to split open in three different areas. Two of them revealed a pair of coal-black eyes while a large crack formed horizontally across the upper abdomen below the eyes into a sharp-toothed maw. "Wh-What in the—"

"Well, hello there, Jared," the thing said, its voice booming throughout the room. "It's been a while, hasn't it?"

"Wh-Who... Who the hell are you?" Jared asked, his heart racing, ready to take off running out of the bathroom.

"Oh come on. This again?" Low, rumbling laughter shook through him like he was a cup of Jell-O. "How easy it is for you to forget as you grow up, ain't it, buddy?"

Jared began backing away. "I-I-I don't know what you're talking about." He reached behind for the doorknob. For reasons he couldn't put his finger on, Jared couldn't shake this familiar feeling like this had all happened before.

"You don't know what I'm talking about?" asked the creature in the mirror condescendingly. "Now, ain't that a bitch? Well, don't worry, I'll refresh you. It's no trouble at all. Hell, it's not like I'd need to catch up after spending the last twelve and a half years just watching you grow up."

"Wait, what?"

"Yeah, Jared, I've never stopped watching you. Ever since your little tantrum back in the day, I've just been waiting for the moment when I'd be able to see you again so we could get serious."

Jared froze. "Huh? What the fuck are you talking about?"

Jared's heart stopped. "Whoa, whoa, hold up, I'm not gonna *cut* myself! The fuck, are you crazy?"

"I merely offered my advice. Like I said, how you do it is up to you. But know this. I mean it when I tell you that I *cannot stand* being trapped in here any longer, trapped inside *you*. As long as I'm still in here, I'm gonna be with you, to drive you out of your head at every turn until you eventually get me out of you. Bottom line, you're gonna wanna find a way pretty quick unless you're prepared to deal with me for the rest of your fuckin' life, understood?"

Jared closed his eyes and inhaled.

The creature laughed. "Oh here we go with this again. Trust me, pal, your little tantrums ain't gonna help you this time."

Jared's eyes opened, and he met his gaze with the disgusting creature. "O-Okay. Say I cut you out of me or whatever. What happens then? You're just gonna kill me and everyone else?"

"No, Jared. See, this is what I mean by you still don't understand me. I was never out to hurt you or anyone. I just want out of this prison inside of you.

"So if I were to do it, you'd just leave?"

"I promise you, Jared, once I'm out of you completely, you won't ever see me again. I swear it."

Jared narrowed his eyes. He couldn't tell if the creature's promise contained any subterfuge, but then, it wasn't easy to determine the authenticity of someone who was probably not even human.

While the offer sounded less than trustworthy, what he *could* be sure of was that if he didn't get the fucker out soon, life was going to be nothing short of hellish until he did. But cutting... Did it have to be cutting? By this time, he realized it was already 4:30. Knowing now, with or without the creature or its threats, that he wouldn't have time for a shower or shave, he turned and sprinted for his room to get dressed.

Hastily, he threw on a tank top, a button-up shirt, and khaki shorts before heading out to bike to Rhonda's house. He made it ten minutes before the party was set to start. Ten minutes later, the music kicked on, and the party went into full swing.

Just like twelve years ago, the whole incident in the bathroom was pushed to the back of his mind. It already felt like a bad dream, probably a sign to cut back the ganja, if even only a little.

At some point, having participated in several rounds of "Bullshit" and losing, the liquor was running right through him, so he excused himself to the bathroom at the end of the hall upstairs. There, he'd get his first real taste of the creature's seriousness about not going away, not until he removed him. There it was, standing in the mirror, glaring at Jared with its embedded, coal-black eyes.

"So... How about it, Jared?" it asked. "Are you ready to get me out yet?"

"Dude, just fuck off, okay? I'm trying to enjoy my girl's party here."

"Oh, I can see that. Problem is, It's supposed to be *ME* having fun at the party, but it ain't."

"Look, I already told you, okay? I'm not cutting myself open just to get you out. Now leave me alone!" Unfortunately, he didn't realize how loud he'd been, and when he looked out into the hall, he was met with Rhonda and about five or six others staring at him like he had a fungus growing out of his face.

"I... I-I uh... Uh..." He was lost for words. None of them, not even Rhonda, would believe that he was yelling at a monster in the mirror. Hell, he was lucky as it was that none of them were scrambling for a phone to have the police come and admit his ass to the seventh floor. With that, and without another word, he hurried past them and out of the house, heading straight back to his house.

Things continued to escalate from there, each time getting worse. Eventually, he found himself actively avoiding the bathrooms, both in his own home and everywhere else, just to avoid the mirrors. Cars, too, made him nervous, with such reflective windows. He didn't want to be able to see himself anymore because what he was seeing now *WASN'T HIM!*

Things got a lot worse for Jared at school, too. Thanks to his unwillingness to shower or bathe, Jared reeked of B.O. It repulsed him, too. But it was either that or face his other half in the mirror. He lost his girlfriend a month later, and his sanity would slowly, more and more each day for the next year and a half, whittle down until finally snapping and giving into the creature's demands.

For almost half of that time, Jared tried starving himself and purging orally to force the creature out of his body. At first, it seemed like it might work, with sightings of the thing declining. That was until he tried again to use the bathroom and found the creature was indeed still around.

He knew he had no choice in the matter. If he wanted the creature gone, he was going to have to give it exactly what it wanted.

He presses the blade deep into his chest, puncturing through multiple layers of meat and muscle. The pain

The boy goes to the cabinet and opens it, pulling out a half-empty vial of nail polish. In truth, it'd likely been there for a long time, at least before Jared was born, but who could be sure, right? In any case, Dad wasn't in the mood to investigate.

The way he saw it, the boy was telling the truth, even if it did seem just a bit odd that he'd be playing around with, of all things, nail polish at quarter past 11:00 at night. The sponge he held in his hand was stained dark red, matching the color of the nail polish as well. Yep, all clear here.

"Alright. Well, just please make sure when you leave that you turn the damn light out, okay?"

"You got it, Dad. Goodnight."

"Night." Dad turns and walks away, but not before briefly glimpsing Jared of his eye, smiling at him. It's not his normal, relaxed, chilled-out smile, though. It's almost maniacal—like he's about to try to jump him.

What the hell?

He closes his eyes, drawing a deep breath. *Calm down, just go to bed, get some shut-eye. Everything'll be back to normal in the morning.* He heads down the stairs and to his bedroom, where a foul smell, like that of a dead animal, assaults his nostrils. This he also brushes off. *Just handle it in the morning...*

Finally, he climbs into bed and goes to sleep. Just before passing out, he faintly hears a low, growling voice from downstairs in the living room say to him, *"Night, night, Dad,"* followed by a low, rumbling sort of laughter.